OCEANSIDE

By

Larry Terhaar

ISBN: 979-8-9900362-0-8 (Paperback)

Contents

FIRST RESPONDERS

JUNE 2021

The alarm tone jarred me awake. A computer-generated voice announced, "Units ten and eighteen respond to building collapse at 88th Street and Collins Avenue." Then the announcement repeated, beginning with the alarm tone. I glanced at the clock and saw it was 1:30 a.m. It was go-time. We had performed this routine countless times over my twenty-five-year career as a firefighter. If it wasn't a real emergency, then we performed timed practices. We needed to be on the engine, ready to roll within a minute. We all slept in natural-fiber underwear that wouldn't melt in extreme heat. I gulped water from the bedside bottle and headed for the pole. The next fifty seconds were automatic, a well-rehearsed routine practiced repeatedly. After quickly checking the landing area one floor below to make sure it was clear, I jumped on the pole, slid down, and immediately cleared the landing for the next guy.

When our shift began thirty-six hours ago, each of us had retrieved our gear from the lockers and methodically placed it in the engine or just outside. As a lieutenant, I rode shotgun, so I had my boots on the ground, ready to step into them before climbing aboard. My turnout coat hung on the door with my radio attached, while my hat, gloves, respirator, and other gear were within reach inside the cab.

Mikey Lopes, already in the driver's seat, had the engine running. The overhead door was already opening as the other four guys climbed into the rear seats. I logged into the Mobile Data Terminal facing my seat with my username: Lt. Dan Crawford. With sirens blaring and lights flashing, we sped south on Collins Avenue. Considering the time of night and our departure from Miami/Dade Station 10, I guessed we would be there in just a few minutes. In typical daytime traffic, it would have taken much longer. As we approached the address, the sight that greeted us was shocking—a drastic change to the skyline we had known all our lives—a building was missing. Behind me were Bruno, Donnie, Jim, and the new kid, Carlos. I could hear their collective gasps. "Holy shit!" Carlos exclaimed.

Visibility rapidly decreased as we neared the scene. Even in the middle of the night, there were enough city lights to illuminate the vast dust cloud that hung where the Oceanside Condominiums used to stand. After a moment, I realized one of the two towers was still standing; the other was just a massive pile of rubble. We were the first unit to arrive. I relayed what I saw to dispatch via radio, and after taking it all in for a few more seconds, I called for a "Full Assignment." This meant that all stations citywide would receive the same alarm we just did and would be on the road within a minute. It also meant that police and ambulances would be on the way shortly.

The Unit 18 Engine pulled in just behind us, which I knew was commanded by Captain Sanchez. Looking at the remaining tower, I could see people on their balconies waving their arms and calling for help.

The magnitude of what I was witnessing horrified me. We had been trained to apply our skills without emotion, but seeing a hundred people screaming for help, I feared there were a hundred more under the rubble. My stomach clenched in a knot, and I recalled the reporter's voice at the Hindenburg disaster crying, "Oh, the humanity."

Captain Sanchez informed me he was taking his team to the standing tower to get those people out. He told me to start searching what was left of the east tower for survivors. I saw the chief arriving in his Tahoe, and I directed Mikey Lopes to take the team and start searching the rubble pile.

The chief approached me and exclaimed, "My God, could anyone have survived?" Chief Williams and I went back a long way. He was my captain for ten years before his promotion to chief. We had worked side by side on too many assignments to remember and trusted each other completely. We could hear more sirens approaching. *Must be the EMTs*, I thought, judging from their distinct sound. I *hope we have some survivors for them to treat.*

"Okay, let's devise a plan," said the chief. "First, we need to shut off the gas. Dan, get on the radio and have dispatch contact Florida Power Utilities to get this gas shut off fast. We don't have a fire so far, and I'd like to keep it that way. I'll call Mayor Santiago," he continued. "We're going to need some excavators here. Maybe he can have Public Works send a couple over. Everyone else, start searching for survivors. Keep your noses alert for gas, and don't do anything that could create a spark!"

I called dispatch on the radio to get them going on the gas company.

We had been on the site for less than two minutes, and our work had begun. Within a few more minutes, a dozen units from other stations started to arrive. I couldn't imagine there would be room for them all to work, but that would be up to Chief Williams to direct. Fortunately, there was room for Unit 20 to park nearby when they arrived. They had the lighting we would need. Besides LED scene lights, they had a bank of lights on a telescoping arm that would put some lights up high above us.

I then joined the rest of my team at the rubble pile, searching and listening for any signs of life. As the other teams arrived, we each worked on a different section of the pile. What used to be a twelve-story building was now just a mountain of broken concrete and steel about forty feet high at the tallest point. It was spread out over the entire lot, which, by my estimation, was about an acre in size. There was still a lot of dust in the air and the grit stuck to my face and in the corners of my eyes. There was a chalky, musty smell that I could taste in the back of my throat, even with a respirator on. I got a call on the radio that an engineer from Florida Public Utilities was on his way and wanted to know how to find me. I told them to have him head for the tallest light and ask for me by name.

Then, I heard from Carlos on the radio. He had located a survivor. As I got closer, I could see he was kneeling over a teen-age girl who appeared to have one leg pinned under concrete and steel. He was checking for signs of life and told me she was alive and breathing but appeared to be unconscious. I called for the EMTs to assist, and two of them rushed over and confirmed what Carlos had reported. The girl had a substantial gash on the left side of her head, and they wanted to get her into the ambu-lance ASAP. The only problem was the pinned leg. I didn't think there was any way we could free her without a machine. Even though we could see only one layer on top of her, concrete and steel were simply too heavy for a few humans to move.

The paramedics bandaged the head wound, set up an IV to keep her hydrated, and put an oxygen mask over her face. Even though she was breathing fine, they wanted to keep the dust out of her lungs. Now, we had to figure out a way to get her free.

At 2:30, we had yet to determine how long until an excavator would arrive. We did have some lifting bags and jaws of life aboard our engine. Perhaps we could figure out a way to put them to use. Recalling that Mikey worked in construction and demolition before joining the fire department, I left Carlos there with the paramedics and went off to find him. He was close by, searching and listening.

"Mikey, I have a situation over here that I'd like you to look at," I said.

"Sure, L.T.," he replied and followed me to the location where the girl was trapped.

"She's alive, but we have to get this weight off her leg soon. I hope we don't have to wait for the excavators to arrive. Any ideas on how we can use the equipment we already have?" I asked.

He got down on his hands and knees and tried to look and feel under the rubble. He got back up and stood there thinking for a few seconds. He looked at me and determined, "I think this one slab is most of the weight, probably two or three tons.

Let's use the lifting bags and lift it enough to clear out the rest and slide her out."

"Okay. You stay here and figure this out. Carlos and I will come back with the bags."

Lifting bags were a relatively new invention to replace hydraulic jacks. The lifting bags were neoprene rubber bags that came in various sizes, and you pump them up with a compressed air tank or a foot pump.

Carlos and I returned to the truck and took out our three medium-sized lifting bags and an air tank. I saw Donnie near the truck and asked him to help us carry the air tank to the girl. On the way back with the equipment, I was reminded how heavy and hot our gear was. Once the sun came up, it would only get worse. I began to think that maybe, at age fifty-one, I was getting too old for this job. Twenty-five years ago, I could have run up the pile and never noticed the weight of our gear. It was a gut punch to realize I was no longer that person.

Upon returning to the girl, the paramedics told us she was stable, and it seemed as if Mikey had a solid plan in mind for using the bags. Just then, I heard over the radio that the FPU engineer was on site and looking for me. I made my way down to the spot where the lights were set up and saw a man with some maps stretched out over the hood of his pickup truck. I introduced myself, and we shook hands.

"I'm Russ Wilson; pleased to meet you." He drew my attention to the maps and pointed out a few spots where they had shut off valves. "How large an area do you want to be shut off?" he asked.

I thought momentarily and replied, "Anywhere we could have broken lines."

He pointed to a spot on the map and declared, "This one here will shut off the whole block, including the remaining tower."

"Perfect," I replied. "How long?"

"Give us five minutes. I have my guys standing by. I'll confirm when it's done, and the pressure is at zero."

"Thanks, Russ," I said. "Let any firefighter know; they can pass it on to me by radio."

I then went in search of Chief Williams. I found him speaking with Captain Sanchez on the west side of the pile. Listening in, I heard them discussing the evacuation of the other tower. His men had already removed the injured people they had initially found. They were now escorting residents down the stairs and outside to gather on the next block south. This was Florida, after all, and many of the residents were elderly. Many had a tough time going downstairs, and some needed to be carried, slowing the evacuation process. The residents were concerned that the other tower could come down, too. So were we.

Chief Williams then addressed the captain and me somberly, "Could a bomb have caused this?"

The question rocked us back on our heels for a moment.

Captain Sanchez said, "We can't rule out anything at this point. Shall I call for the bomb squad?"

"We have to. Make the call, but not over the radio; too many people have scanners these days, and we could create a panic."

"Will do," the captain said.

The chief exclaimed, "While you're doing that, I'm going to call the mayor again and see if we can get someone from the building department down here for a look and bring the blueprints for these buildings."

As Captain Sanchez walked to his truck to use his phone, I got word over the radio that the gas had been turned off. The chief heard it as well.

"Thank God," he said. "Good job, Dan."

I told him about the girl we found and asked him if there was any word on when we would see some excavators. He said, "The mayor promised two by daybreak, but I'll try to confirm that again." It was now three a.m., and there was still too much dust in the air to go without respirators.

It seemed that all the first responders in Miami were on the scene. The deputy fire chief, most of the police department, and more EMT ambulances than I knew existed were here. By now, many senior firefighters were on the scene—those ranking higher than me. I knew I'd have to watch how I communicated with Chief Williams to respect the chain of command.

THE DEVELOPERS

SUMMER/FALL 1979

My name is Jack Brooks, and I am the founder of New Florida Consultants, Inc. I specialize in development consulting in the State of Florida, assisting real estate investors, developers, builders, and civil engineers in advancing their projects. With a focus on working with local municipalities and their commissioners and zoning departments, my job was to obtain project approvals. Over the past five years, I have developed a substantial client base and earned a reputation for success.

Originally from New York, I was raised in Brooklyn and attended school there. My first job was with a civil engineering company that worked with developers doing site plans for subdivisions on Long Island. Besides doing the technical work, our firm was hired to represent the developers and builders at local zoning and health department meetings. Much of our work involved securing zoning variances. If one of our clients wanted to build something in an area not zoned for that use, we would apply for a variance. We would try to get that zoning classification changed to one that would allow our clients' buildings to be built.

Here's an example: getting a property in a residential single-family zone to be changed to multi-family housing or getting a condominium built on a property zoned as light industrial. Sometimes, we would work to re-classify the whole area. Sometimes, we applied for a variance for a single parcel, claiming a hardship specific to our client's project. We would accomplish this by advocating for our clients using our relationships with the zoning commission members. Some might call this schmoozing, but I find that word unappealing. It was more like just getting to know them personally and gaining their respect. While in their offices, I would always be professional, upbeat, and friendly. Other times, I would just stop by to say hi or offer them tickets to a baseball or football game. These relationships were built over time.

When necessary, my boss would use his political influence. Occasionally, he used his relationship with elected officials to advocate for our clients. Sometimes, political influence meant campaign donations. Sometimes, it meant projects that benefitted the town or city that the politicians could take credit for in their campaigns. Sometimes, it was providing a block of votes, such as a union or another organization. Occasionally, it was an inside opportunity to invest in a venture likely to succeed financially. There were ways that the most connected could influence elected officials.

In 1978, a United States congressman or senator received a salary of $61,000. How could they have afforded one of the nicest houses in town, an apartment in Washington, first-class air travel, and expensive suits? There exists another level of business in this country that benefits both businessmen and politicians. The company I worked for had established a reputation for obtaining project approvals using any means available.

Following one successful zoning change application, the client, Gary Rosen, invited me for a beer to celebrate after the evening zoning meeting. During our conversation, he said he was considering moving his business to southern Florida. According to Gary, that was where the real money was being made. Waterfront land could be purchased for peanuts and developed into 100-unit condominiums. You could buy land just a mile inland and build 300-home subdivisions. He told me that the municipalities loved growth and would provide water, sewer, and paved roads. This was fueled by property tax revenue, the jobs produced, and local prosperity.

Gary wanted me to come with him, perhaps as an employee or a partner. Or maybe, he suggested, I should think about opening my own consulting business down there, and he could be my first client. I was intrigued. We discussed the idea a bit more and agreed to meet again in a few days.

It was a lot to think about. Perhaps Florida was the opportunity of a lifetime. I was only twenty-nine years old at the time and had no wife or family. At 6'1" and 185 pounds, with a full head of dark hair, I was still in shape for lacrosse and brimming with confidence. Ultimately, I had nothing to lose. I had saved a little money, at least enough to get settled and hang up a shingle, and I already had my first client lined up.

The following week, when we met, I told Gary that I was interested in following him down there and setting up shop. I had done some research, and it seemed to be just as he described. He said he was getting ready to move to Fort Lauderdale and hunt for an opportunity, and he'd let me know when he was settled and needed my help.

Within four months, Gary called and told me about a property he had bought. It was right in Fort Lauderdale between A1A and US1. He was working with a civil engineer who thought two hundred single-family homes could be built there, including some on a canal with ocean access. The engineer had other clients interested in investing in the project, so Gary was off and running.

I gave my boss in New York a month's notice and made plans to move to Florida. I wanted to get down there as soon as possible to start building a relationship with the municipal officials. Packed with everything that could fit in my Mustang, I headed south.

Gary was renting a house on a canal in the middle of Fort Lauderdale. He told me I was welcome to stay with him until I found my own place. When I arrived, he took me on a tour of the town and then to see the property he had bought. While walking the property, he warned me to watch out for snakes, which was never something of concern on Long Island!

After that, he took me down to the beach. Beautiful. I was immediately taken by the local girls in bikinis. It was a way better scene than back in New York, and we both knew we would love it down here.

So that's how my life in Florida began. After a week, I found a small storefront on Las Olas Boulevard to rent as an office. It had an apartment upstairs where I planned to live. However, I was in no hurry to move out of Gary's. He constantly had a stream of girls coming by to swim or sun by the pool. Sometimes, they would spend the night. I was loving life in Florida.

After a month of partying at Gary's, it was time for me to get to work. This was the first time in my life that I didn't have a boss to answer to or regular office hours to keep, and I realized I would need to discipline myself with a daily work routine;

otherwise, going to the beach and chasing pretty girls would be too tempting. Each morning, I would plan my day by listing goals and accomplishments and working that into a schedule of appointments or phone calls to be made. I would then coordinate that with a monthly planner to keep track of deadlines and commitments.

I moved into the apartment on Las Olas and set up my office. Then, I met with an attorney Gary recommended and filed my corporation documents. My next order of business was to get to know everyone I could at City Hall. I would go down each day and introduce myself at different offices. While there, I would hand out my business cards and try to get to know the officials, and I stopped by the zoning office at least once a week.

I met with Mike Graves, the civil engineer Gary was using. He informed me that it would be another month until they would be ready for me to start filing the various applications. In the meantime, he introduced me to some of his other clients. My pool of contacts was growing.

Gary's project, "The Moorings," went through all the permitting without a hitch. There were no special efforts required. He offered me one of the homes at cost, and I took him up on that offer. It would be a few years until I moved in and ultimately gave up the apartment and office on Las Olas, as it had become apparent that I was doing all of my business either on the phone or in someone else's office.

Through some of the contacts I made through Mike Graves, I worked on projects from Boca Raton to Miami. I was getting to know all the land use departments in two counties. I felt pretty proud of myself, and whatever doubts and fears I had about coming to Florida and starting a business were now in the rearview mirror.

In the summer of 1979, I was contacted by Howard Stein regarding a project that his group wanted to do on North Miami Beach. He had bought a two-acre beachfront parcel zoned for apartments or condominiums up to three stories high. But his vision for the property was a twelve-story, 200-unit high-rise. I met him in Miami one afternoon, and we walked the property. The whole area was pretty much undeveloped. There was one three-story condo a few blocks north of his parcel. He told me that upon his first inquiry, the land was zoned for three stories because the bedrock was thought too soft to support anything more. He told me Mike Graves thought a high rise could be built with modern soil testing and construction techniques. We chatted a bit longer and agreed to speak again soon. I told him I would be happy to help where I could.

The following day, I stopped by Mike's office to get the story from an engineering standpoint. He told me that most of the bedrock down here was a soft sedimentary rock called coquina, especially on the barrier islands. He explained that it was comprised of limestone, coral, and other organic materials like shells.

He remarked, "You're from New York. Have you noticed that all the high-rise buildings in Manhattan are located on the southern end and in midtown? That's because that's where the bedrock is granite. It will support a near-unlimited amount of weight. Other areas of Manhattan have softer rock and won't support as much."

"I have noticed that," I admitted. "But I never fully understood the reason."

Mike explained, "We now have some proven engineering methods to build on top of softer rock that will support more weight. It requires excavation on site to expose the rock and then testing the strength. After that, a structural engineer can design the footings accordingly."

I asked him if this was something we could demonstrate to the building officials.

"Yes. Plenty of data is available from other places where this was done."

"Okay. Now that I know what we're dealing with, I assume you've discussed this with Howard?"

"Yes, I have. He wanted to get you onboard so the three of us could put a plan of attack together."

"Okay, I'll reach out to Howard and ask him how he'd like to proceed."

I spoke to Howard later that afternoon and told him about my discussion with Mike. I asked him if he had already lined up an architect or a structural engineer.

"Brian Comstock and Associates have a structural engineer on staff. They've done a good job for me in the past."

I offered to go to City Hall in North Miami and see if they were open to a presentation from us.

Howard agreed. "Go ahead. Let me know how you make out."

The following morning, I drove to North Miami and walked into City Hall. I thought I might get shuffled between departments, so I started with the zoning office. At least I had gotten to know them and was on a first-name basis with them. I asked to see Don Jacobs, the zoning enforcement officer. After being invited back to his office and exchanging a few pleasantries, I told him about the project on the beach. I knew the parcel number, and he located it on his map. He informed me that it was zoned for a three-story building. I told him I knew that and explained what we wanted to build and why we thought the ground would support it.

He looked at me questionably and asked, "Are you certain of that?"

I relayed my discussion with Mike and said, "We won't know until we test it."

He considered it momentarily and stated, "Well, you'll need both a zoning change and a sign-off from the building department. They will probably want a sign-off from engineering as well."

I asked him where I should start.

"Well, put in a zoning application, and while you're waiting for that, I would ask the building department if they would consider the testing you propose. In the meantime, I'll get with the rest of the zoning board for an initial finding to get you on the schedule."

I thanked him for his help and asked about his kids and family before leaving his office. He told me that he had taken his kids to a Marlins game the day before, and they had a great time. I picked up the zoning applications at the counter on my way out. Next, I went down the hall to see the building inspector, Jim Waters. He was kind enough to see me, and I repeated my conversation with Don down the hall. I inquired if they were open to recognizing our testing method. He told me they'd done it before, but he would need to consult with engineering before giving me a firm "Yes."

"Would you like me to speak with engineering directly?" I asked.

"No, I have a meeting with them after lunch and will bring it up then."

I thanked him for his time and headed out. That was about all I could accomplish there that day. Next, I needed to meet with Howard again to complete the zoning application and await the building inspector's reply. This was a Friday, so I planned to call Howard Monday morning.

When I got home, I had a message from Gary waiting for me. When I returned his call, he invited me to join him and his girlfriend, Judy, for dinner on Saturday. He told me that Judy would bring a friend who wanted to meet me. Okay, we'll see how that goes, I thought. I had met Judy a few times at Gary's, and we got along well. She was quite attractive and a good conversationalist; we always seemed to be laughing when we were together. I was expected to meet them at Gary's house at six p.m. for cocktails, and we'd all go out from there.

When I arrived on Saturday, I found everyone out by the pool. Judy introduced me to Michelle, who was stunning: long dark hair, a beautiful face, impeccable makeup, and a little black dress that showed off a fantastic body. Michelle told me she had heard so much about me and was glad she was finally meeting me. Uh oh, I'm in for it now, I thought. I wasn't used to being set up on a date and initially felt some trepidation.

We all chatted for a while, getting to know each other. Michelle told me she worked with Judy at the law office as a paralegal. I found speaking with her easy, and my earlier apprehension eased. If only I could keep my eyes on her eyes while talking to her.

We rode in Gary's car to the Huke-Lau, a new Polynesian restaurant that was very popular. Judy sat with Gary up front, with Michelle and me in the back. She sat close enough to me that I could faintly smell her perfume.

The Huke-Lau was a South Pacific-themed building with an open-air feel amid tropical gardens and waterfalls. We crossed a wooden bridge over a running river to get to the entrance and were seated in the corner with some privacy, but we could still see the novelty surrounding us.

"Don't you just love this place?" Michelle asked.

Gary and Judy agreed.

Feeling a bit embarrassed, I replied, "This is my first time here."

I had a feeling that Judy and Michelle had done the planning for this evening. The ladies ordered two Mai-Tais served in hollowed-out pineapples for the table, each with two straws.

Michelle and I shared a drink, and Gary and Judy shared the other. With the sounds of birds in the background, we continued the easy conversation and were having a good time. I felt very comfortable around Michelle. We ordered a Pu-Pu platter as an appetizer, along with Kalua pig and sweet and sour shrimp to share. It was delicious; I hadn't had anything like it before. We drank more Mai-Tais, and feeling their effects, I lost track of how many.

After we finished the meal, Judy suggested we "go back to the house for a swim."

We all agreed and climbed into the car. Michelle sat next to me, and I wrapped my arm around her. She purred in my neck, and I turned her face toward mine, kissing her. She kissed me back with encouragement and continued to nuzzle my neck the rest of the way to Gary's house.

When we entered the house, Gary asked me to help him in the kitchen with the drinks. He asked what I thought of Michelle. I answered, "What's not to like? She's beautiful!"

When we returned to the pool, the ladies were already in the water, naked, with only the underwater pool light illuminating their bodies. We set the drinks down near the pool, and Gary and I stripped off our clothes and joined them. Soon, I realized Judy had led Gary to one end of the pool, leaving Michelle and me at the other. We gravitated toward each other, and moments later, she wrapped her arms and legs around me. She kissed me passionately, using her tongue while we sucked on each other's lips. I became increasingly aroused. She reached down, guiding me inside her while my hands cupped her ass.

Just a couple of hours ago, I only hoped to go home with a phone number, and now we were having sex in the pool. We stayed the night in Gary's guest room and made love a few more times. At this point, I just assumed I had "gotten lucky" tonight. I had no idea who I just met.

We slept until nine the following day and joined Gary and Judy for coffee and bagels in the kitchen. The ladies silently communicated with each other, and when they weren't looking, Gary and I low-fived behind the counter.

It was Sunday, and no one was in a rush to leave. We lounged around the pool for the rest of the morning—this time in bathing suits. Michelle looked just as fine in the daylight as she did last night. Around one p.m., I announced it was time for me to go, and I thanked Gary and Judy for being great hosts. As Michelle walked me to the door, she handed me a slip of paper with her address and phone number written on it. Then, when she put her arms around my neck and kissed me, pressing against me, I could feel myself becoming aroused again.

"I'll call you soon," I whispered.

"You better."

I went home to tackle the laundry that had piled up during the week. All I could think about was Michelle. In an attempt to distract myself, I went outside and washed my car, but it didn't help.

I contacted Howard on Monday morning and scheduled an appointment for the following morning at his office. Later, Jim Waters, the building inspector, returned my call and informed me that they were willing to recognize the testing but requested that we let them know when we planned to do it so they could observe the test. That was good news from the building department. Now, it was just up to zoning. We were making incremental progress!

Despite attempting to focus on my work for other clients, my mind kept drifting back to Michelle. I didn't know what it was about that girl, but I was starting to think my preoccupation was about more than the sex. Not wanting to wait until tonight to call her at home, I contacted Gary.

"Hi, Gary," I said when he answered. "I'm calling to get a phone number for the law office where Michelle and Judy work."

He gave me the name of the law firm and the phone number.

"Oh, one more thing. What's her last name?" I asked.

We both laughed before he replied, "Maxwell."

"Thanks, pal," I replied and then ended the call.

I wrote down the number and re-thought if I should wait a day or at least wait to call her at home that evening. I decided to wait until four, then call her at the office and invite her to dinner. I managed to focus on work for the rest of the afternoon. At four, I called Michelle's office number.

"Michelle Maxwell, please," I said to the receptionist.

"Who should I say is calling?" she asked.

"Jack Brooks," I replied.

"Hold, please."

Michelle came on the line and proclaimed, "Jack! I'm glad you called. How's your day going?"

"Great," I replied. "How about yours?"

"Same old, same old."

"I was hoping you might be available to grab dinner with me tonight," I said, trying to sound as casual as possible.

"I'd love to. What do you have in mind?"

What a loaded question that was…. I decided to leave it alone.

"Have you been to the 15th Street Fish House?" I asked.

"Yes, I love their conch salad."

"What time should I pick you up?" I asked

"How about seven?"

"Perfect. I'll see you then."

I tidied up the house in case we ended up here later. I changed the sheets and cleaned the bathroom. I showered, shaved, and dressed, picking out my favorite shirt.

While driving to Michelle's, I realized I had butterflies in my belly, something I hadn't felt since high school. When I rang her doorbell, she answered, wearing a loose-fitting silk outfit that provocatively draped over her breasts.

"You look fabulous," I remarked.

"Oh, this is just something comfortable I've had for a while," she said, hugging me. We kissed, still standing inside her door. "Would you like to come in for a drink before we go?"

"With the way you look. I'm not sure we'll ever get out of here."

She smiled and agreed. "Okay, let's go then. I'm hungry."

On the way in the car, I inquired, "So tell me about yourself. Where did you grow up? Where did you go to school? I want to know everything."

She told me she was from Minnesota, the middle child of three with two brothers, and had attended the university there. She explained that she came to Florida five years ago to take a job at the law firm.

We sat by the window overlooking the docks when we arrived at the restaurant. She commented, "This is lovely." After our drinks were served, she asked, "So, tell me about you."

I told her about growing up in Brooklyn, working with the land use company, and coming here a few years ago with Gary to start my consulting business. She asked if I was ever married. I told her no and that while I had some relationships in school, nothing serious ever came of it. I told her I had dated a bit since being in Florida, but nothing serious.

"How about you?" I asked.

She revealed that she had been in a serious relationship in Minnesota. "After a couple of years, our interests just started to grow apart," Michelle explained. "I think that's when I started looking out of state for a job. And as a girl from freezing cold Minnesota, when I got a job offer in Florida, I was here in a heartbeat."

The waitress stopped by our table and asked, "What can I get you two?"

We both ordered the conch salad as an appetizer and shared an order of grilled Mahi—the fish of the day. I ordered a bottle of chardonnay as well. As our appetizers arrived, I asked Michelle if she'd had any relationships since being in Florida.

"No," she claimed. "I've been on a few dates, but I find most of the guys here insincere. The ones I dated seemed like they hadn't grown up since high school. All they talk about is fishing." Then she said something I wasn't expecting. "The other night with you was the first time I've had sex in five years." She laughed. "Maybe that's why I was so horny!" She laughed again, then covered her face with both hands in embarrassment. "I can't believe I just told you that!"

I confessed, "It's also been a long time for me."

"Oh, you're just saying that to make me feel better."

"No, it's true. I've been completely focused on building my business for the last few years."

Our fish came, and we put the plate in the middle of the table for two and shared it. When we were done, we held hands while finishing our wine. "Would you like to come see my house?" I asked.

She considered it momentarily and said, "I wouldn't be able to spend the night. I'll need all my things to get ready for work tomorrow. How about you come back to my place?"

"Ready when you are."

After another sip of wine, she said, "I'd love to see your house, though. Maybe on a weekend?"

"Does this weekend work for you?" I asked.

"It does," she replied.

"Friday it is then."

"Cheers!" we exclaimed as we touched glasses.

When we arrived at her apartment, and I opened her car door, she stood and kissed me. She led me by the hand into her house, directly to her bedroom. She lit two candles and started unbuttoning my shirt. We made love just as hungrily as the first night at Gary's.

After recovering, she put on a long gown tied at the waist, and I pulled on my pants. We went to her kitchen, and she made us decaf coffee with a splash of Bailey's and placed a small plate of dark chocolate on the table. We kissed and touched and kept admiring each other between sips of coffee. When we were finished with dessert, she led me back to her bedroom, and we were passionate again, but this time more slowly, experimenting with things we hadn't done with each other before.

When we were both spent, we lay in each other's arms for a long time before either spoke. I was afraid to say anything because I wasn't sure if she was feeling the same way I was.

Finally, she said softly, "Are you feeling how I'm feeling?"

"Oh my god," I whispered. "Absolutely."

We both laughed and squeezed each other harder.

In the morning, I awoke to the sound of a hair dryer from the bathroom. I could see it was 6:30 by the bedside clock. I lay there, recollecting the events of the last forty-eight hours. Eventually, Michelle came out of the bathroom wearing the gown she'd worn the night before, with her hair done and makeup on.

She sat next to me on the edge of the bed and kissed me. She told me she needed to leave for work in a half hour and asked if I wanted breakfast.

"Just coffee would be fine."

We kissed some more, then she stood and went to the kitchen. I got dressed and followed her. Over coffee and fruit, we made plans for the weekend.

"How about I drive to your house after work on Friday? I can be there by six," she offered.

"That would be great. I'll make us dinner."

"I'm looking forward to it."

I wrote down my address and phone number on a notepad I found on her kitchen counter. She followed me to the door, put her arms around me, and we kissed again. Then, it turned into more than a kiss. I knew she could sense my arousal, and I suspected she knew exactly what she was doing.

"You better go," she sighed, "or I'll never get to work."

While I was preparing for my meeting with Howard back at home, Don called and stated that the commission had given us conditional approval. He explained that the conditions were: 1) we get through the public hearing with approval, and 2) the building department approves our testing and engineering. The public hearing was scheduled for the first Tuesday in August.

If it sounds as if we were making progress, we were. But the public hearing would be the big stumbling block. We all knew the pitfalls of a public zoning meeting. We would need to post a notice on the property and invite all the neighboring property owners to attend. This must be done by certified mail to prove to the zoning board that everyone was notified. When Howard and I got together later that morning, I told him about the building department and the initial finding from zoning, as well as the public hearing.

"Good news. I'll let Mike know."

While Howard and I were working on the zoning application, we realized that we would need some preliminary drawings at some point before the meeting. I was sure that we would need to submit a footprint plan along with the application.

"Well, I guess it's time to get Brian started on the plans," Howard said. "At least enough for the zoning application."

He called Brian and put him on speakerphone. He told him I was in his office and told him about our progress. Brian suggested that we just do concept drawings for now.

"You'll need those for bank financing, and they'll cover anything zoning needs as well," he explained. "We won't go to the expense of the full drawings until you have the zoning permit and have done the testing, so we'll know what the bedrock will support. Give me a week, and I'll have you over to look at the preliminaries."

"Sounds good," Howard said.

Brian added, "Fax me a list of the number of units, targeted price range, and the amenities you want to include."

Over the next week, Brian put together the preliminary drawings, Howard and I finished the zoning application, and I returned to Don's office to submit everything. I thanked him for all his help and asked if he'd like four Marlins tickets. I explained that something came up and I could not use them, while actually, I had bought them purposefully for him.

"Sure, my kids would love to go to a game," he said.

On Wednesday, I worked for my other clients and checked in with Gary to see how his newest project was progressing. He filled me in on it and then mentioned, "Judy tells me you and Michelle are still hot and heavy."

I remarked, "Oh, I'm sure she'll just love to hear it described like that."

We both laughed.

"Would the two of you like to join us again for dinner on Saturday?" he asked.

"Sounds good to me, but let Judy ask Michelle. I'm not sure what her plans are."

"You got it," he said as we hung up.

So this is the way it's going to be, I thought to myself; anything I did with Michelle would get back to Gary via Judy. I'd need to keep that in mind. The rest of the week, I thoroughly cleaned the house and even shopped for art to hang on the walls. All of a sudden, I cared how the place looked.

On Friday, I went grocery shopping. I wasn't sure what to cook, but I had only seen her eat salad, fruit, vegetables, or seafood whenever I was with her. I went to a fish market and bought two halibut filets. I had a recipe for pan-seared halibut with a lemon beurre blanc sauce. I thought I would serve it with fresh asparagus. I bought a small chocolate decadence cake for dessert and bagels for the morning at the bakery. I stopped at the liquor store and bought two bottles of a Washington State Pinot Gris that I liked. It was now late afternoon, and I was already getting butterflies.

I showered, shaved, and put on shorts and a polo shirt. I searched through my music collection for something that would fit the mood. I felt like a schoolgirl getting ready for the prom, and the butterflies were back.

At six p.m. on the dot, the doorbell rang. I opened the door to see Michelle holding a small overnight bag. It looked like she had gone home after work and changed; she was wearing shorts and a tank top, and I was struck by her beauty once again. I guided her in the door and closed it behind us. She set down her bag, and I took her in my arms, giving her a big hug.

She looked around and commented, "This is nice. I was wondering on the way over what your place would be like. I like it."

"Let me make a couple of vodka martinis, and I'll give you the tour. Would you like yours with an olive or a twist?"

"Olive, please, just a little dirty."

She followed me into the kitchen, taking in the whole place. The house was a typical Florida ranch. From the kitchen, it was all open to the dining and living areas, with a quadruple sliding door overlooking the patio and backyard. The bedrooms were on the other side of the foyer. When I prepared our drinks, I handed one to her, and we both took a sip.

"Shall we?" I said.

"After you," she replied.

I led her through the dining room to the living room. She stopped and said, "Let me drink this down a little bit. I'm afraid I'll spill it walking around." She took a big sip and concluded, "Mmm, I needed that."

We went out the sliders to the patio overlooking the back-yard. She nodded approvingly at the big yard with citrus trees and a fence surrounding it. Back inside, I led her down the hall past the guest bath and a couple of bedrooms, one of which I used as an office. When we got to the primary bedroom, she put her drink on the nightstand and pushed me down on the bed.

She climbed over me and said, "I've been waiting for this all week." Our clothes came off, and we made love with her on top the whole time. She took complete control of her climax and then mine. After a while, we disentangled and resumed sipping our martinis. Once we caught our breath, I asked if she was hungry.

"Starving!" she replied.

I put my shorts back on, and she took one of my dress shirts out of the closet and put it on. She giggled, "I've always seen this in the movies—the girl wearing her lover's shirt after sex."

We returned to the kitchen, and I opened one of the bottles of Pinot Gris. I poured two glasses. "Cheers!" we exclaimed once again and took a sip.

"Oh, I just love this," she said, picking up the bottle to inspect the label.

"It'll probably take me fifteen minutes or so to cook dinner. Would you be more comfortable in the living room?" I asked.

"If you don't mind, I'd like to stay here and watch you cook."

"I don't mind at all."

Having already rinsed the fish and trimmed the asparagus, I started on the sauce. It needed time to cook while I did the rest. I put some oil in a skillet and heated it while putting some water in a pot to steam the asparagus. When the water was boiling, I dropped the asparagus into the pot and put a lid on it. I set the timer for two minutes and stirred the sauce. When the oil was good and hot, I slid the halibut into the pan, and it immediately started to sizzle. I added salt and pepper to the fish and stirred the sauce again, dropping in butter cubes. When the timer went off, I removed the asparagus pan from the heat and turned off the burner. I then turned the halibut over, revealing the golden sear I had hoped for. I reset the timer for another two minutes, then stirred the sauce and drained the asparagus. I placed the asparagus on the center of the plates. When the timer went off, I put the halibut on the asparagus and drizzled the sauce over the top.   "Voila! Dinner is ready."

Michelle appeared mesmerized. After a moment, she exclaimed, "I've never seen anyone prepare a meal like that before. You were like a conductor leading a symphony!"

I modestly replied, "Well, I hope you like it."

I carried our plates out to the table while Michelle brought the wine. I pulled a chair out for her and then sat down opposite. "Dig in," I offered.

She took a bite and marveled, "Oh my God." She looked at me and took another bite. "This is the best piece of fish I've ever had."

She was silent for the next few moments as she ate. After a few more bites, she set down her fork and exclaimed, "And he can cook, too! I think I'm falling in love."

We both laughed initially but then looked deep into each other's eyes momentarily. I smiled, "Can we finish eating now, please?"

"Absolutely," she laughed.

After dinner, I asked, "Would you like dessert on the patio?"

"Sure."

We stood up and carried our plates into the kitchen. I handed her some matches and asked if she would go out to the patio and light the citronella candles while I brought out the dessert. "Would you like some coffee as well?" I asked.

"I'm enjoying this wine," she told me as she headed toward the patio.

I put a Marvin Gaye record on the stereo, then went back to the kitchen to slice the cake. I carried it out along with what was left of the wine bottle and left the slider open so we could hear the music.

She invitingly patted the chair next to her. "Sit close to me, Jack."

I did and placed the cake plates on the table. "I have another bottle of this," I offered.

"I'm fine for now. I don't think I've been this content in a long, long time."

"Me too," I agreed.

We sat there holding hands, just listening to music, along with the crickets and other creatures that live in southern Florida. After a while, I started working on my cake.

She took a bite and said, "This is yummy." After another bite, she asked, "Could we go back to bed now?"

I took a moment to cover the candles, went inside, turned off the stereo, and dropped the plates back in the kitchen. When I reached the bedroom, Michelle was already in bed with the covers pulled up. I could see my shirt hanging on a chair. I went to the bathroom, brushed my teeth, and climbed into bed with Michelle. After making love again, we slept the night in each other's arms.

We both stirred when we sensed the sun starting to rise; she got up and went into the bathroom. I could hear her brushing her teeth. She returned to bed and made love to me while the sun came up.

I went to the kitchen a while later to make coffee. While it was brewing, I put the dishes in the dishwasher and cleaned up a bit. When she came in, she was wearing my shirt again. I poured the coffee and put out cream and sugar, along with bagels and cream cheese.

After she had a sip of coffee, she said, "Last night's dinner was the most wonderful meal I've ever had. Do you always cook like that?"

I laughed. "No way. Cooking for you was a special occasion. Usually, I'm just a sandwich guy, and I don't get too carried away cooking for myself."

"Good to hear. If you keep cooking for me like that, I'll gain twenty pounds," Michelle laughed.

After spreading some cream cheese on a bagel, I asked her if she had spoken to Judy about going out tonight.

"Yes, she did mention it, but I told her I would have to discuss it with you."

"Well, do you want to?"

"Not really," she replied. "I just want the two of us this weekend."

"Sounds good to me," I said, kissing her forehead as I walked by to get more coffee. "What would you like to do today?"

"Maybe go to the beach. I brought a bathing suit."

"That's what we'll do then. I'd like to see you in that bathing suit," I said suggestively.

"Not much suit to see."

"Then we're definitely going!"

"May I use your phone to call Judy?" she asked.

"Certainly. It's right there on the wall. Or you can use the one in the bedroom if you want some privacy."

"This one will be fine," inferring she had nothing to hide.

While she was calling Judy, I packed a few soft drinks, a few beers, and a bottle of wine in a cooler and got some beach towels. When Michelle finished her call, she grabbed her things, and we headed to the beach in her Volkswagen Scirocco. When we arrived, I rented a cabana with some lounge chairs. Once we had all our stuff arranged, she slipped off her cover-up. She was right. It was a pretty tiny bikini, just some strings and small triangles of fabric. I thought of that popular song from twenty years ago, but hers had no yellow polka dots.

As we enjoyed the day, I did notice people walking by to get an eyeful. I couldn't blame them. After a few hours, we started to get hungry. "Are you thinking late lunch or early dinner?" I asked.

"How about we pick up some Chinese on the way back to your house?"

"Perfect. I know just the place."

She slipped her cover-up back on, and then we packed our things and headed to the car. It was about 5:00 when we got back to the house. I put the Chinese food in the oven to keep warm and joined Michelle in the shower. We soaped each other up but didn't let it get too romantic. Then, we brought the food out on the patio, paired with a couple of beers.

We chatted about our lives and growing up. She told me about her brothers and everything they did together, like skiing and ice fishing. That triggered a regret I always carried, and I told her I wished I had a brother to play sports with. We talked about how we saw our futures. Subconsciously, we may have been feeling each other out to see if there was room in our futures for each other.

We continued talking for a while, then went into the bedroom and made love virtually all night, pausing to sleep occasionally. I woke up once around four and thought to myself that this woman was too good to be true. I started to wonder if it was all a dream. I snuggled into her and fell back asleep. When we finally woke up together, we smiled at each other, feeling something special was happening. We hugged each other tight and wouldn't let go. Eventually, sensing the bright daylight outside the drapery, I glanced at the bedside clock. It read 10:00, and I started laughing. When she looked at the time, she laughed along with me. We both typically would have been up for hours by now. I threw some shorts on, and we made our way to the kitchen. While the coffee was brewing, we discussed what to do for the rest of the day.

We decided to go window shopping on Las Olas and maybe find a spot for lunch. After wandering up one side of the street, the aroma of freshly baked bread led us into a little Parisian café. Our conversation took us into a deeper understanding of each other's lives over a flute of champagne and a warm ham and melted cheese baguette.

Conversations like this usually occur before people become physically intimate, but that was not true for us. We stayed for coffee while our soulful conversation continued.

When we walked down the other side of the street, I bought Michelle a necklace she had pointed to displayed in a shop window.

After returning to my car, I asked, "Would you like to go back to the house?"

She took me by the arms and turned me to face her. "Jack, I'm sore. We can't have any more sex for a few days."

"That's okay, honey. How about we just take a nap?"

"Only if you promise to be good," she said. "Otherwise, I could go home."

"I'll keep my hands off you. I promise."

She giggled. "It's not your hands I'm worried about."

We returned to my house and slept, cuddled in each other's arms. I realized I needed some recovery time as well.

When we woke up, Michelle sighed. "I've been dreading this moment, but I think it is time for me to go."

I took her in my arms. "I loved this weekend."

We looked each other in the eyes, and she kissed me. "Me too."

We hugged for another minute before I helped her carry out her things. I watched her drive away, wondering if my life had just changed.

The following morning, while sipping my coffee, I got a call from Howard. "What can we be doing to prepare for the zoning meeting?" he asked matter-of-factly.

I told him what my plans were. "Usually, I'm fearful of the neighbors at one of these meetings. Everybody complains about having to look at a monster building that will block their view and ruin the neighborhood. But in this case, our only neighbors are other landowners like you. I'm pretty sure it's in their financial interest that we get approved."

"I see exactly what you mean and couldn't agree more," he said. "If we get this through, the value of their property doubles overnight."

"For sure. So, I thought I'd contact each of them to check if they're on the same page and see if we can count on their support."

"Great. Have we sent out the notices yet?"

"I did that on Thursday," I replied. "Now, the next question for you is if you're interested in making a political contribution to the mayor's campaign. The election is three months away."

"Another good idea, Jack. The timing couldn't be better."

"With our meeting scheduled before the election, we only need to support the incumbent mayor. How much would you like to donate?"

Howard thought momentarily, then offered, "I think ten grand would get his attention and not break the bank."

"That sounds about right to me. I'll contact his campaign manager and set up a meeting."

After we hung up, I poured myself more coffee and made a bacon and egg sandwich. As I sat down to eat, my thoughts wandered back to Michelle. I am usually an all-business guy, but I couldn't get her out of my mind.

I forced myself to focus and called the mayor's office, asking to speak to the campaign manager. I was told he didn't work out of that office, but I was given his name and a phone number to reach him. I called the number and asked for Mark Johnson.

"Hold, please."

I waited.

"This is Mark," he said when he came on the line.

I introduced myself and explained that I wanted to meet him to discuss a contribution to the mayor's campaign. I'm sure he knew exactly why I was calling and what I was after.

"That would be great, Jack. My calendar is open tomorrow all afternoon."

We agreed to meet at 1:00.   I couldn't start contacting the neighboring property owners since they probably hadn't received the notices yet. As I thought about my next step, thoughts of Michelle took over, so I gave in and called it a day.

The following morning, Howard called again and told me Brian had some drawings for us. I explained I had a meeting with the campaign manager at one o'clock and asked if we could go to Brian's that morning. He said it was already set for 10 a.m. and that we should meet there.

When I got to Brian's office, he and Howard were standing over the table, looking at the drawings. Howard asked him about the cost to build and the projected selling prices.

"Let's take a seat over here. I've printed out some numbers for you."

He handed us both a proposal folder that read "Oceanside" on the cover and walked us through the numbers. "Okay, at the current cost of construction of $60 per square foot, the units will cost between $50,000 and $120,000 each to build. If you recall, you told me you wanted a variety of floor plans, from one bedroom to three bedrooms, plus some larger units as penthouses."

"That's correct," Howard replied.

"I would project the selling prices of the units to be between $125,000 to $250,000. And maybe more for the penthouses. That's at today's market prices. By the time you get these on the market, those numbers will likely be higher. The projected profit should be in excess of one million dollars."

"I love it," Howard exclaimed. "Jack has a meeting this afternoon to try to grease the wheels at City Hall," he told Brian. "Let's hope this zoning meeting goes in our favor."

We all shook hands, and I headed to Miami on US 1.

Mark's office was in the new tower next to City Hall. The lobby was impressive, with a marble floor and light maple wood accents. I pressed the elevator button for the twelfth floor.

He was very welcoming and ready for me when I arrived at his office. I guess when you're coming to donate money, everyone is welcome. He invited me to sit at his conference table and asked how they could help. I told him about the "Oceanside" project and the impending zoning meeting in two weeks. I explained the zoning issues we were facing and hoped to have changed, detailing how the engineering plan would make it doable. I added, "If the mayor could come out publicly in favor of the project, it would be a big help."

"Certainly. The mayor is always in favor of more tax revenue and more jobs."

"In exchange, we would like to donate $10,000 to the campaign."

"Well, I'm sure you know we can't promise a quid pro quo, but if you were to make that donation, I'll make sure he knows who it came from and inform him of your project."

"Who shall we send the check to?" I asked.

"The Francis T. Mathers re-election campaign, in care of this office," he answered and handed me his card. I told him the check would go out in the morning mail. I rose to leave, and we shook hands as he walked me out.

"Mayor Mathers will be very appreciative of your generous donation."

I stopped in the lobby to use a pay phone to call Howard with the news, the payment info, and the mailing address.

"I'll get that out this afternoon," Howard said. "Nice job, Jack."

I headed home with nothing remaining to do the rest of the day. Thoughts of Michelle returned to mind during the drive. I could not understand how someone like her could not have already been taken. When I got home, I decided to call Gary. When he answered, I asked, "Do you have any time this afternoon? I have something non-business related to talk to you about."

"Sure, anytime. Is this about Michelle?"

"Oh, you're such a wise man," I teased.

"See you soon," he chuckled.

On the drive over, I made a mental list of the things I wanted to discuss.

When I arrived, he invited me in and cracked some beers to take out by the pool.

"Gary, you're the only longtime friend I have down here. I met this girl a week ago, and now I can't get her out of my head."

"Wow. That's pretty fast."

"I know; that's why I'm here. I just can't understand how a beautiful, smart, sexy girl like her could still be available. Is there something in her past I should know about?"

"Nothing I'm aware of, and I've asked Judy as well," he replied.

"I mean, I have good instincts regarding my work. I can imagine the pitfalls in advance and prepare for them if they occur. But with her, I am doubting my instincts."

He asked, "These business instincts that you have, do you feel them in your gut?"

"I do," I replied.

"And you trust them?"

"Absolutely."

"I recommend you also trust your gut instincts about her." After a moment, he pulled a piece of paper from his pocket. "Let me show you something. Michelle asked Judy these same questions about you. Judy wrote them down for me to answer."

He went on to read the note: How could a handsome, successful, loving man make it to thirty-four years old without someone scooping him up? Is there something in his past he hasn't told me? Was he ever in prison?

He handed me the note. While I read it over again, Gary brought out two more beers.

"Let's keep that note between us. Judy would kill me if she knew I shared it with you."

"Will do. So you think I shouldn't worry about it and just trust my gut?"

"Yes. I've known you a long time and never seen you like this over a girl. Judy is close to her. She has known her long enough that if something were off, she'd know it. Judy also told me that Michelle has never been promiscuous as long as she's known her. She was surprised at how she behaved with you."

"Thanks, Gary," I said, relieved. "You've made me feel a lot better."

"I'm not advising you to marry her after a week, but enjoy her and see how it works out."

"You're a good friend, thanks, man." We did a bro-hug, and he walked me to the door.

"Let's do that dinner with the ladies. I'd like to get to know her as well," Gary stated as I headed to my car.

I felt like a weight had been lifted from my shoulders, and I was pleased to hear that Michelle was doing her own "due diligence." It was starting to seem as if maybe she was "the one."

When I got home, I went into the kitchen and made a sandwich, carefully layering the ham and cheese and adding both mayonnaise and mustard. Then I took it into the living room to eat in front of the TV. Michelle was still on my mind, and I wished she was here. At seven p.m. I couldn't stand it and called her.

"Hi, Jack. I'm glad you called."

"Hi, honey. I've been thinking about you. How are you feeling?"

"Still sore." She laughed. "I'll be better soon. Don't worry."

"I'm not worried. I just wanted to hear your voice."

"Do you want to come over on Friday again?" I asked.

"Yes," she replied. "I'm sure I'll be fine by then."

We laughed. "Okay then, I can't wait to see you!"

"Great. Good night, Jack."

"Good night, Michelle."

The following day, I called the neighbors in North Miami Beach to whom we had sent the notices. I reached a few of them and left messages for the others. The people I contacted confirmed receiving the notifications and asked about our plans. I offered to come to meet with them. Most just wanted an explanation over the phone. Of the ones I contacted, they told me we would not get any objection on their end.

The day after that, I drove down to show the plans to another neighbor. He also said he would have no objections. Some people I left messages for called back, and I reviewed it over the phone. Again, I heard no objections. One claimed he thought it would be great to get the zoning changed.

"You might make me a rich man!" he exclaimed.

I called Howard to let him know the favorable response I was getting from the neighbors.

After listening, he said, "I'm not surprised, but I'm still relieved to hear it. Thanks, Jack."

There were two more neighbors that I hadn't spoken to yet. I was sure I would reach them in the next week.

I was looking forward to seeing Michelle that night. I stopped and bought what I would need to make Chicken Parmigiana along with ingredients for a salad. I also bought a couple of bottles of Montepulciano. After showering and shaving, I had time to prep the chicken, so all I would have to do later was stick it in the oven.

Michelle arrived a little after six, and we went straight into each other's arms when she entered. At that moment, I realized how much I had missed her all week and wondered if this was what falling in love felt like.

"What can I make you to drink?" I asked.

"That martini you made last week was great."

"Coming right up."

I made one for each of us and carried them carefully into the living room, sitting beside her. I could tell she had just showered and washed her hair; she smelled and looked beautiful. We talked about our work weeks for a little bit, and I told her I had dinner all ready to put in the oven. "What, no show tonight?" she said with a big grin.

"Well, you can watch me make a salad."

"How about you watch me make a salad?"

"I'd love to," I answered as we strolled into the kitchen with our drinks.

I put the chicken in the oven, and Michelle began to rummage through the refrigerator for some salad makings. I took a large salad bowl out of a cabinet for her, then sat down at the counter to watch her work. She was pretty comfortable in the kitchen, and I suspected she was a good cook. While we waited for the chicken, I opened a bottle of wine and poured us each a glass.

"To us!" she toasted.

"To us!" I replied.

When we sat down to eat, and after tasting the chicken, she declared, "This is excellent!"

"So is the salad," I said. "I just realized I've never seen you eat meat."

"Oh, I eat chicken all the time. I'm just not into big slabs of beef."

After dinner, we took our wine onto the patio, and I lit the citronella candles.

"Jack, why don't you have a pool?"

The question took me by surprise. "Well, I've only been here two years, and when I bought the house from Gary, it was about all the money I had. I've been filling it with furniture ever since. With no one here to enjoy it, I never saw the need."

She sipped her wine and asked, "Do you remember the first night you met me?"

"I'll never forget it," I replied.

"We could do that again if you had a pool."

"We'll go pool shopping tomorrow." I laughed.

"Maybe one with a jacuzzi, too," she added, laughing as well.

When we went to bed that evening, we were hungry for each other and made love repeatedly throughout the night.

I slipped on some shorts and went to the kitchen in the morning. As the coffee was brewing, I walked back to the sliding doors, gazing at the backyard. I was imagining where a pool would go and how it would look. Michelle joined me and put her arms around me from behind.

"What are you looking at?" she asked.

"I was just imagining a pool back here."

"It would be nice," she agreed.

We returned to the kitchen, and I poured us coffee. She went into the refrigerator and took out the cream. She was getting comfortable at my house.

As we sipped our coffee, I asked, "Shall we go pool shopping today?"

"Really? You sure don't waste any time, do you?"

"I guess not. How about we visit those model homes we always see advertised? I'm sure we'll be able to check out some nice pools the way they have those places all decked out."

She thought a moment and agreed. "That's a fantastic idea. I love exploring those places, and you could get some good ideas."

"We could get some good ideas. Let's get dressed and go."

"Give me a little while. I'm a mess and need some time to get ready."

"Take all the time you need. It's the weekend."

I tidied up the kitchen and brought things in from the patio while she dressed. When she emerged, looking fabulous again, I smiled and said, "My turn."

After getting dressed, I grabbed my little Minolta camera and checked it for film. We got in my car and drove to a new subdivision I'd passed on the road frequently. There are always "Model Homes" signs along the road, including directions for parking and signs pointing to the models. Upon entering the first one, we had to sign in. I signed us in as "Mr. and Mrs. Brooks." As we strolled through, Michelle commented on things she liked about the decorating. I listened closely and wondered if she would be doing the rest of the decorating at my house.

We made our way to the pool area. Nothing special about this one. It was small and very close to the house. The next model we visited had a larger pool with an integrated Jacuzzi elevated slightly, creating a waterfall as water flowed into the pool. There was also a large screened enclosure that encompassed the whole patio.

"This is wonderful," Michelle said. "I love the Jacuzzi."

I took a few pictures as we inspected it more closely. On the way out, business cards were on a counter from all the vendors who supplied decorating for this model. I pocketed one that read "Rizzo Pools."

We both liked the pool at the next one; it was kidney-shaped, with a round Jacuzzi tucked into one side of the small end and a staircase on the other. This design of the stairs created a spiral.

"That's interesting," Michelle commented. "I like that."

I took some pictures of it as well. We decided to tour the rest of this house. Michelle pointed out things she liked and didn't like, and I paid attention. Walking back through the house, we passed the counter of business cards. I noticed the "Rizzo Pools" card on this one also. I pointed this out to Michelle and said, "I guess I should call Mr. Rizzo."

She nodded her head.

We walked through the last model, and this one didn't have a pool at all. The host stated they could add any pool we wanted. Walking back to the car, I asked Michelle what she thought of the screened enclosure we saw.

"I like it," she said. "It keeps the bugs out and the pool clean. I've been seeing more of them lately. They call it a cage."

I asked her if she wanted to try to find some more model homes.

"I think we have a pretty good idea of what we like."

We drove back to the house to get cleaned up for our dinner plans with Gary and Judy. I quickly showered and dressed, then went into the kitchen to make drinks. Michelle took quite a bit longer. When she came out of the bedroom, she looked fantastic. She was in a little red dress that reminded me of the black one she wore when I met her for the first time.

I told her that, and she replied, "Thank you. I'm glad your memory is good for two weeks!"

We laughed, and I handed a drink to her. She took a sip and said, "Yummy." I loved it when she said that.

Gary and Judy picked us up at seven p.m. for the twenty-minute drive to the restaurant. It was great for Gary and me to get together when it wasn't about business. Upon arriving at the restaurant, I noticed the decor was all white, gray, and chrome. And lots of glass. Michelle commented that it felt beachy but without the driftwood and sand. We were seated by the window, and after ordering a bottle of chardonnay, we continued our conversation from the car.

When I mentioned we were considering putting in a pool, Gary said, "You have to use Steve Rizzo. He's the best, and I'll tell him to give you the builder's price."

Michelle and I laughed and told them about picking up his card at the model homes we had seen and liked his work.

We had an enjoyable meal and great conversation, with everyone laughing throughout the evening. After dinner, when they dropped us off, Michelle and I went straight to bed. We snuggled together, enjoying the comfort of each other's bodies, and made love slowly and tenderly.

Sunday was another beach day, and she wore a slightly more conservative bikini that would at least allow her to go in the ocean without the surf tearing it off. She drove herself home that night for another work week. After seeing her off and entering the house, I felt melancholy. I missed her already and imagined what being married to her would be like. As my mind led me down that path, I also feared endangering the way we were together now. I concluded it was best to take this slowly and not scare her off.

When I went to sleep that night, that was on my mind.

Monday morning, Howard called and informed me that Brian had completed the finishing touches on the plans, and everything was ready for me to submit to the zoning office. I told him I would pick up the plans from Brian and deliver them today. He went on to ask if I thought we should go ahead with the soil testing.

"I think so, Howard. The engineering probably won't be finished in time for the zoning meeting, but we might as well get it scheduled."

"Go ahead and schedule it then."

"I'll be in touch," I said and hung up.

I was able to get everyone scheduled to do the testing on Wednesday. I updated Howard and notified Jim Waters, the building inspector. He told me he would stop by the site late in the morning.

I also called Steve Rizzo and made an appointment with him to come to the house on Saturday at ten o'clock to discuss the pool.

On Wednesday morning, I drove to Miami to meet Mike and his soil testing crew. Fortunately, the weather was perfect for working outside: cloudy with no rain and not too hot. Along with Mike, there was a machine operator with an excavator and another guy with an air-powered core driller. The air power came from a compressor that was towed behind a pickup. Brian's engineer, Dave Culver, showed up, and we talked while Mike directed his crew where to dig the holes.

Mike explained how the test worked. "We'll dig holes with the excavator at about ten places on the property. Once we're down to the coquina, we will take a core sample to be brought back to a lab. The lab guys will place the core samples in a press and apply pressure until the sample is crushed. The amount of pressure it takes to crush the sample will tell them the strength of the rock. Dave here will use that data in his design accordingly."

Around eleven o'clock, Jim Waters showed up to observe our testing. He watched us work for half an hour and asked Mike to forward the data to him, along with a map showing where the holes were dug. Mike agreed, and Jim left. There wasn't much for me to do, so I offered to bring back lunch for everyone. I went to a local deli and ordered sandwiches that we ate on the tailgate of the pickup. When I left at one o'clock, the guys were about sixty percent done with the testing. Mike said they should be able to finish today.

When I reached the house, I called the remaining property owners we had sent notices to. Both were happy that we were paving the way for high rises on the island. Like the others I spoke to, I asked if they would attend the meeting to show their support. They both agreed and wished me luck. Then, I drove to Brian's office to pick up the plans and returned to Miami to deliver them to the zoning office.

I stopped into Don's office while I was there. He thanked me for the Marlins tickets and confessed he had a lovely day at the park with his sons. "Are you ready for the meeting next week?" he asked.

"I think so. "Any tips for me?"

"You'll be fine. I can tell you've done this before."

"Thanks for the confidence, Don." We shook hands, and I left his office.

Michelle came over on Friday. I made chicken cacciatore and garlic bread. We had another bottle of the Montepulciano that I knew she liked.

She exclaimed, "Jack, you're killing me here. I will not look like this if you keep feeding me such wonderful food. You're the best cook ever!"

When we finished the wine, I asked if I should open another bottle. She responded, "Jack, please take me to bed. I've missed you all week."

When we got into bed, she raised herself on her elbows and looked me in the eyes. "I love you, Jack Brooks."

"I love you, too, Michelle Maxwell."

We made love passionately that night. We had finally said out loud what we had been feeling all along.

In the morning, I got up to make coffee while Michelle dressed. She joined me in the kitchen, wearing shorts and a tank top, and we had breakfast while we waited for Steve Rizzo. When he came to the door, I introduced him to Michelle and told him about the pools we had seen at the models. We strolled around the backyard as Steve observed the sun's positioning.

"It looks like the house will partially block the afternoon sun, so I recommend extending the patio on the far side. I think you will want the equipment on the side of the garage so you won't have to listen to it all day. Is the electric panel in the garage?"

"It is."

"Perfect. Are you thinking about a full enclosure?"

"We are."

We sat at the table, and he opened up his picture book. "Here is a pool we designed and installed with the extended patio I mentioned."

Michelle and I liked what we saw. He then asked what kind of patio surface we wanted and showed us more pictures of our options. We both gravitated to the natural limestone.

"I'm assuming you want a Jacuzzi as well?"

"We do."

"Do you want it in the pool or separate?" Steve asked as he showed us more pictures.

After reviewing the different styles, Michelle stated, "Either in the pool or very close. We'd like to go back and forth without walking any distance."

"Okay. Do you like a rectangle or free-form?" he asked, pointing out pictures of each.

"Free-form," we both exclaimed at the same time.

"And lastly, do you want a waterfall or other water feature?" Again, he showed us some examples.

"I'm not sure. What do you think, honey?" I asked Michelle.

Before she answered, Steve offered, "Something to consider is the sound of a waterfall. Some people love it, and some people end up hating it."

"I like quiet," Michelle stated.

"There you go," I concluded.

"I'll work up a quote for you with a design. I should have it ready for you in a few weeks."

"That's great. It seems like you know what you're doing."

"Thirty years, Jack. I've built it all."

As we walked him out, I asked if he had done any other pools in the neighborhood.

"The Moorings? I do all of Gary's pools."

"You know Gary?" I asked.

"Ever since he came to town."

I told him about my relationship with Gary and that I did all the permitting for his projects.

"In that case, you'll get the same price I give Gary."

"Wonderful, thanks for that. I look forward to seeing what you come up with."

"Sure thing, Jack. I look forward to working with you two. Good day, Michelle," he said as he walked to his truck.

We walked back inside the house, both giddy with excitement. I was happy that he offered me the builder's price without me having to ask for it or for Gary to intervene. We returned to the patio to imagine how the pool would look. "This is going to be fantastic!" Michelle exclaimed.

"That it is," I added.

We went out to dinner that evening, and after returning home and relaxing in bed, I felt so lucky to have found Michelle. I loved everything about her and no longer felt fulfilled unless I was with her. I knew I wanted to marry her.

Sunday turned out to be cloudy and a bit windy. We were disappointed that it wasn't a good beach day, but we ended up going to Gulfstream Park to watch the horse races. We had a lot of fun. We had lunch overlooking the track and left fifty dollars ahead. Upon returning to the house, we both became melancholy. She didn't want to go, and I didn't want her to leave either. I had recently been thinking about asking her to spend Sunday nights with me, but I was afraid I would be pressuring her, so I decided to wait for her to bring it up.

While Michelle gathered her things, she suddenly cheered up and said, "I can't wait to see what Steve comes up with."

"I'm pretty excited, too."

We kissed, and she thanked me for a wonderful weekend before getting in her car and driving away.

On Monday afternoon, Howard called to tell me that Mike had completed his testing data and forwarded it to Brian and Dave. They had done the engineering calculations with those results and would have a summary ready for us to submit at the meeting tomorrow evening. He said one of them would attend the meeting to assist with the presentation.

I was growing more optimistic about the meeting every day. I spent most of Tuesday making sure I was prepared for anything that could come up. This was when the worries set in. What if one of the neighbors objected after all? What If one of the environmental groups caught wind of it and sent people to protest? I ran into these problems in New York, so it was natural for me to worry about them. It was up to me to deal with these issues; I was hired to do exactly that.

The meeting was held in a small auditorium-styled room with the board members at a long desk in the front of the room. When the meeting started, Don Jacobs introduced all those in attendance. He then put a projection of our site plan up on the screen. I made the primary presentation to the board, showing them what we wanted to do and why we thought it was appropriate for the site. I then asked Don to put the architectural rendering on the screen. There seemed to be a favorable reaction to the appearance of the building, and it was then that I mentioned the Mayor's public support. I then turned the meeting over to Brian, who explained the results of the soil tests and how, through proper engineering, the bedrock would support our project. He also noted that the building inspector had observed our tests. When we were done, Don asked if there were any objections to the zoning change. There were none. I naturally became anxious, and I could feel my heart rate increasing as the board huddled together for nearly ten minutes. When they appeared to be finished deliberating, they handed Don a slip of paper.

"Approved!" Don announced finally.

My heart started to beat at its regular rate again as we filed out to make room for the following item on the agenda. Brian and I shook hands, and I went down to the pay phone to call Howard. He was equally overjoyed. When I walked to my car, I thought, That was easy. This is why I moved to Florida.

On the drive home, I reminded myself of the fee I would earn from this project. I could easily pay for the pool and still have money to buy Michelle a ring. I knew Michelle wanted to hear the results of the meeting, but by the time I got home, it was after ten p.m., so I decided to call her at the office in the morning.

When I did, she said, "I'm so happy for you, Jack. I know you worked so hard on getting it approved."

I told her I would have no problem paying for the pool now, and she was happy about that, too. I let her go because I knew she had work to do. The rest of the week was uneventful. Michelle came over on Friday. We chatted while I cooked dinner, and after, we made love pretty much all weekend.

The following week, I decided I would ask Michelle to marry me. I went to the library and read everything I could about diamonds. I needed to know everything; that's just the kind of person I am. I learned about the various cuts, qualities, and carats. I hoped I would understand a jeweler's terminology and ask the right questions with some knowledge. I went to a few stores for ideas and a feel for pricing. I discussed making a custom ring at one store where the jeweler seemed honest. He showed me all the possibilities. I chose a high-quality one-carat round cut, surrounded by ten smaller diamonds in a white gold band, with a total weight of two carats. He asked me what her ring size was.

"Uh-oh!" I laughed. "I have no idea."

He said not to worry. He'd make it in a popular size I could have re-sized later, and it would be ready in a week. I was so excited, I was walking on air. I knew this was a big deal—something I hadn't imagined just a month ago. I hoped she would like it. I hoped she would say yes!

Having that behind me, I could now focus again on work. I had the zoning approval, so the next step was getting the building permit for Oceanside, and we were waiting for Brian to finish the plans. In the meantime, I could work on the water and sewer permits and meet with Florida Power and Light. Brian told me we would use gas for heat and hot water, so I met with Florida Public Utilities to get the ball rolling for a gas hookup. I called Don Jacobs at the zoning department and asked him if there was any type of environmental permit we needed since we would be working this close to the beach. He told me they had yet to get that far with the environmental stuff, but he would appreciate it if we put up a silt fence before we started digging to protect the dune. I called Brian to get a rough timeframe for when the plans would be ready to be submitted. He said we would be good to go in two more weeks.

Lastly, I called Howard to tell him what I was working on and asked if I missed anything. He said he couldn't think of a thing. He said he would be sending me fifty percent of my fee for getting through zoning. I thanked him for that. The last fifty percent would come when the building permit was issued. I had nothing left to do, so I took the rest of the day off. Naturally, my mind went to Michelle as I tried to think of something special for the proposal.

The following day, after walking a property with Mike Graves, he took me to lunch at a marina where he kept his sport fishing boat. While eating, I was admiring a sailboat docked next to where we were seated, and it dawned on me: What if I charted a sailboat for an afternoon and proposed on the boat? I shared this thought with Mike, who told me of a sailboat captain he knows at the marina that does charters. After lunch, Mike and I strolled down the dock to meet his friend, Captain Hans.

I told the Captain what I had in mind, and he said he had done dozens of proposal charters and had even performed a wedding ceremony at sea. We made arrangements for Saturday afternoon, giving me just two days to get my courage up!

When Michelle arrived on Friday evening, we immediately jumped into bed and satisfied our lust that had been building all week. After we recovered, she followed me into the kitchen wearing my-her shirt. While we sipped on cocktails, she watched me make my version of Pad Thai. I casually suggested, "How would you like to have lunch on a sailboat tomorrow?"

"Really, where?"

"At the marina where Mike keeps his boat. There is a Captain that does half-day charters; I met him earlier this week, and he said he has Saturday open."

"Sure, that sounds great. I've always been intrigued by sailboats."

"Well, that's good to hear because I already booked it!"

After we enjoyed our spicy dinner, we sat on the patio as a gentle breeze kept us cool and fantasized about our future pool again.

The following day, we slept until nine, and I put on a pot of coffee and toasted a bagel for us to share. The phone rang while we were enjoying our breakfast.

"Hello, this is Jack."

"HI Jack, it's Steve Rizzo. I have your design completed and am wondering if you have any time tomorrow for me to come by?"

"Great, Steve; we've been looking forward to it. How about one o'clock?"

"That's perfect, see you then. Bye, Jack."

"Bye, Steve."

Michelle had overheard the whole conversation, and I could read the excitement in her eyes.

We hopped in my Mustang at eleven-thirty and drove to the Bahia Mar Marina. We parked the car, and as we headed for the dock, a breeze caused Michelle's long, dark hair to flow behind her. When we reached the dock, I said, "The name of the boat is Eclipse; see if you can spot it."

We strolled down the dock, looking at the names. "There it is," she pointed to a navy blue-hulled boat about forty feet long with two rolled-up white sails.

"Hi, Jack, welcome aboard!" we heard as we approached. I introduced Michelle, and he said, "I'm Captain Hans; we're all ready for you."

"Wow!" Michelle exclaimed. "Your boat is beautiful."

"Glad you like her." He smiled while giving us a hand aboard. "Please put your shoes in this basket and make your-selves comfortable." He then busied himself, preparing for our departure. The Captain was tall, thin, and weathered; I guessed around fifty-ish. A young lady walked up the steps from below and handed us each a glass of champagne. "I'm Ava; I'll assist Captain Hans this afternoon."

"Hi, Ava, we're pleased to meet you," Michelle replied.

With her youthful face and sun-bleached hair, Ava appeared to be in her early twenties. "Would you like a tour below before we get underway?" she asked.

"Sure," I replied.

We went down a few steps, carrying our champagne, into the "salon," the living quarters below deck. There was a seating area around a table and a small galley kitchen. Forward was a bathroom, also known as a "head," and a sleeping berth in the bow. There was another sleeping berth in the rear, opposite the galley. It all looked quite comfortable.

When we returned to the cockpit, Captain Hans acknowledged, "I see you've met my daughter, Ava; she'll be preparing lunch for you today."

Michelle and I looked at each other, imagining we were in for something unique. I asked, "Is there anything I can do to help you get underway?"

"No, thanks. Ava and I can handle it all. You two just sit back and enjoy."

He started the engine, and he and Ava untied the lines. When we were out of the slip, Ava pulled in all the fenders, and we headed out of the inlet. She stowed the fenders under the seat opposite us and pointed out the life jackets there as well. Once we were out in the ocean, they rolled out the sails and turned off the engine. It was now quiet, with just the sound of the waves running past the hull. This was the magical part of sailing for me. We were traveling silently without machinery running, just by harnessing the wind.

Captain Hans told us, "We'll just head downwind for now while you have lunch. After that, we can go anywhere you want."

It was a glorious day, with clear, deep blue skies contrasting with the white tips of the waves. Ava refilled our champagne glasses and set out formal plates and silverware. Michelle looked at me in wonderment. Our first course was chilled cucumber and dill soup. It was delicious. When we finished that, Ava served us fresh grilled Mahi with mango chutney and saffron rice.

Michelle asked Ava, "Did you make all this down there?"

"Mostly, although I must admit to doing some prep work at home."

"It's wonderful; I never thought you could eat like this on a sailboat."

When we were done, Ava asked, "Would you like an espresso or just stick with the champagne?"

I answered, "Espresso, please, we don't want to miss any part of this experience."

Michelle hugged my arm, and Ava asked if we would like any sugar or anisette with it.

"Anisette, please," I replied.

Ava served us the espresso and set a small bottle of anisette on the cockpit table with a plate of Italian cookies. She then went back below. Michelle again looked at me with amazement.

When we were nearly finished with our dessert, Captain Hans set the autopilot and said, "Excuse me for a minute; I need to go below and prepare things for sailing upwind."

When he was gone, Michelle kissed me and confided, "This is the most romantic day I could ever imagine."

"It is nice, isn't it? I'm glad you like it."

I reached into my pocket, took out a little jewelry box, and got down on one knee.

Michelle shrieked, "Oh my god!"

I opened the box, and she exclaimed, "Yes, yes!"

After a considerable kiss, she looked at the ring and added, "I love it!"

"Try it on, let's see how it looks."

She slipped it on her finger, extended her hand admiring it, and again exclaimed, "I love it, and I love you!" She kissed me again.

I guess the captain had a good sense of when she had calmed down. He and Ava returned with more champagne and exclaimed, "Congratulations!"

Looking at me and laughing, Michelle realized the whole thing was a setup, and the Captain and Ava were in on it. Ava refilled our champagne glasses and took our espresso cups below.

Captain Hans asked, "Which way would you like to go, Admiral?"

I laughed and replied, "How about up the coast? Let's get her moving."

"Aye, aye," he acknowledged as he and Ava started trimming sails while he turned us northward.

Eclipse started to lean over, and Michelle held me tighter. We were flying now. Once Michelle was no longer clinging to me and was more comfortable with the boat's attitude, Captain Hans asked me if I would like to take the helm.

"Sure, just stand by in case I mess it up."

"I'll be right here," he assured me.

Steering a big boat, heeling over, and going fast was fun. Michelle was looking at me, wondering how I knew what to do. After about ten minutes, I asked her if she wanted to try.

"Sure, but Captain, don't you move!"

He assured her, "I'll be right here, no worries."

We changed places, and I took another sip of champagne. She was doing very well, holding a steady course. The captain gave her some tips on anticipating waves, and she immediately got a feel for it.

After a while, Captain Hans told us, "It's time to turn south. Would you like to steer us through the turn, Michelle?"

"Sure, if you show me how."

"I'll talk you through it."

Ava got ready to adjust the sails, and Captain Hans instructed Michelle to turn to the left. As she did, the boat slowed, and then when the boom slowly swung to the other side, the ship started to lean the other way. Ava began trimming the sails on the other side, increasing our speed.

"Okay, hold this heading. Nice job, Michelle."

She was grinning ear to ear.

After a few more minutes, Captain Hans told her, "I'll take it from here; you go enjoy your champagne with your fiancé."

She looked at me and laughed, "Fiancé? That's the first time I've heard that word referring to me!"

We continued to sit with my arm around her, sipping champagne all the way in. Michelle was fascinated with every move Ava was making while taking in the sails and preparing for docking. We thanked them for a beautiful day once they had Eclipse tied up and shut down. I slipped an envelope to the Captain, and we stepped off the boat.

"Congratulations!" we heard as we walked down the dock.

As we approached the car, Michelle stopped and leaned against the hood. She looked at me and exclaimed, "Jack, that was the most wonderful day of my entire life; I love you so much."

I hugged her, and we kissed. As she was opening her door, she let out a joyous shriek, "I can't believe we're engaged!"

Once we were on the road, I asked her if she wanted to stop anywhere to eat.

"No way, take me home and make love to me. And hurry!"

The following morning, we slept late, then lounged for a few hours, drinking coffee and reading the paper while Michelle admired her ring. At one o'clock, when Steve arrived, we sat at the dining table because it was too hot to be outside. Once we were seated, he noticed Michelle's ring and asked her if it was new.

Michelle replied proudly, "Yes, Jack just gave it to me yesterday."

"Congratulations to both of you; it's a beautiful ring."

He took out a sketch of the pool he had designed for us. It was exactly what we had hoped for: a free-form pool with a Jacuzzi at one end and a large extended limestone patio, all in a fully screened enclosure. He then showed us an itemized proposal with everything we requested. I was pleased with the bottom line number, as he had given us the builder's price because of my work with developers. Then he asked if we had any questions.

I replied, "How soon will it be completed?"

He told us it would be six to eight weeks if we gave him the go-ahead today. I wrote him a check for $10,000 to get started.

"We'll start pulling permits right away." As he left, he said again, "Congratulations, you two."

Over the next couple of weeks, Michelle would come over on the weekends, I would cook dinner, and we would enjoy every moment together. She would go home on Sunday nights, and we would both work all week.

Then, finally, one morning, Howard called and told me that Brian had finished the plans. It was now time to apply for the Oceanside building permit. I made an appointment with Jim Waters for Brian and me to go to his office to review the plans. He asked that the structural engineer be there as well. I called Brian and told him about the appointment, informing him that Dave was needed.

On Thursday morning, the three of us met with the inspector in his conference room, where we could spread out the plans. This inspector was very thorough compared to many I had previously worked with. He wanted to go through the plans page by page and ask questions. We started with the foundation plan, and he questioned Dave about the soil and footing calculations. Dave was ready with all the data and all the answers. When we reached the garage level, he asked Dave about the columns.

He stated, "You have columns in an area where cars could strike them. What happens if a car takes out one of the columns?"

Dave replied, "Good question. First, a car would be destroyed long before it could take out a column. But let's imagine if a heavy truck could get down there. If any of these columns are removed, even an end one, these beams above will spread that load to the rest of the columns, and it will not fail."

The inspector thanked Dave for his thorough explanation. We went on to the next floor. On each page, he had more questions. It took us until one o'clock to complete the review.

We walked out of there with the permit in hand. The three of us were overjoyed. No one understands the complexity of getting a building approved, especially a big one on the beach, requiring a zoning change. We called Howard from a pay phone with the news.

"Hallelujah!" he cheered. "Nice job, you guys."

After hanging up with Howard, I called Michelle.

"Congratulations, Jack. I know how big of a deal this is for you."

I was grinning from ear to ear on my way out of City Hall. The construction of Oceanside was about to begin.

THE RESIDENTS

We lived in Westchester County, New York, in the house where we raised our two sons. Hannah, my wife, had just retired from a career as a school teacher, and over the past year, I had been winding down my real estate career. We'd been contemplating what to do for the upcoming winter. Our kids were grown and out of the house, so nothing was keeping us here. We had often talked about retirement plans and lately had both expressed interest in spending the winters someplace warm.

Hannah said, "We can visit my sister in Fort Lauderdale for a week or two."

Her sister, Lori, and her husband, John, had retired a few years ago and moved to a new home on the Intracoastal Waterway. They had a dock and kept a boat in the backyard—a center console fishing boat with two 400-horsepower outboards. John claimed it would go 65 MPH.

"Should I give her a call?" asked Hannah.

"Sure, sounds good to me."

Hannah picked up her cell phone and dialed her sister. They started with the usual sister-to-sister chat, catching up on the kids and family stuff. I then heard Hannah say, "Bob and I were wondering if you guys would be up to having us down sometime after the holidays?"

I could hear Lori's excitement through the phone. "Absolutely! Yes!"

I got up and went into the kitchen to prepare dinner, letting Hannah work out the details with her sister. I took some shrimp out of the freezer to thaw and then mixed up a batch of Cosmopolitans—Hannah's favorite cocktail. When she was done with her call, I guess she heard me shaking the drinks because she asked, "Is that what I think it is?" as she walked into the kitchen.

"Of course. So when are we going?"

"She wants us to come for the whole month of January."

"Really? Won't that be too much of an imposition?"

"That's what I said, but she insisted."

"Cheers!" I said while we touched our glasses. "After dinner, I'll look at some flights."

"Perfect, I am so looking forward to this."

While I prepared the scampi, Hannah turned on the six o'clock news. The kitchen was open to the TV room, and regardless of who was cooking, we spent this time together each evening. Ever since our boys were grown and out of the house, I prepared dinner one night a week—the whole thing, including the dishes. This gave Hannah a break from preparing every meal, every day, as she had done throughout our marriage.

We fell in love at a young age and had been together for almost all our adult lives. We were high school sweethearts and married as soon as we finished college—actually, I am a year older, so it was when she finished college. Speaking for myself, I never wanted to be with another woman. Curious, sometimes, but never giving it more than a passing thought. I always assumed she felt the same about me and our relationship.

I had just turned sixty-one and thought we had done well to be able to retire comfortably, still young and healthy enough to travel and enjoy life. While I was getting a little thicker around the middle, I still had a full head of sandy-colored hair, but if you looked closely, it was half-gray.

Along with our two wonderful sons, we have two grandsons, both in elementary school. While we were watching the news, the scent of garlic filled the air, signaling the scampi was almost done. When the timer went off, I plated our shrimp along with a salad.

We sat down to enjoy our meal as the news changed from local to national. Lately, the new president had dominated every headline. Hannah and I have never been political; sometimes, we didn't even vote. But we were dumbfounded as to how this guy could have been elected. Being from the New York area, we had been aware of him for years. He always seemed quite the braggart and publicity hound. Everyone knew he had bankrupted two casinos and stiffed his contractors. He bought an airline, which quickly failed, along with the Plaza Hotel, that went bankrupt. He had borrowed massive amounts of money from all the New York banks and defaulted on the loans. In addition, he was a skirt chaser and was now on his third wife, having cheated on all of them. Not exactly the kind of man you would want to be president. While I hoped things worked out for the country's sake, I had doubts. The truly alarming thing to me was that enough other people didn't see what we did. We vowed to pay more attention to our civic duty and vote next time.

After cleaning up from dinner, I sat down at the computer to check on flights.

"Things are pretty nuts between Christmas and New Year's," I commented, browsing the internet. "JetBlue has a few affordable flights on the third; will that work?"

Again, she said, "Perfect!"

I printed out our tickets: Robert and Hannah Osborne. We went to bed that night feeling excited about our upcoming plans and made love with renewed energy.

For the holidays, we had our kids and grandkids over to the house for our usual Thanksgiving feast, our tradition for over thirty years. We lived in a grand old house in a storybook neighborhood, built in the twenties, that we had completely renovated over the years. For Christmas, we went to our older son Matt's house, where we shared Christmas through the eyes of children, which made our day magical. As the new year approached, we started packing for our trip and made a list of things to do before closing up the house for the impending cold weather.

WINTER/SPRING 2018

On the third, we had a smooth, on-time flight direct from White Plains to Fort Lauderdale. When we stepped outside the terminal, the humidity hit us immediately, something I had noticed on previous visits, along with the distinct smell of the tropics. Lori and John met us outside baggage claim, whisking us off in their new Toyota Highlander.

I asked, "Hey, should we rent a car while we are here?"

"No need. We have an extra car. You can either take this one or the Jaguar convertible. John still has his Mercedes," Lori replied.

Upon reaching their new home, we were immediately impressed by the curb appeal. While getting the grand tour, we saw how lovely a new, modern home can be. This one was designed to let the outside in. From the moment you walked in the front door, your eyes led you through to the pool area and, beyond that, to the boat dock and the water. After the tour, we sat by the pool with some drinks while watching the boat traffic on the ICW.

"This is the life," I said. "The pictures do not do it justice."

"I just love it!" added Hannah.

"It sure beats the winters in New England," said John. "Moving down here is the best thing we have ever done."

Lori was two years older than Hannah. She and John had been married almost as long as we had. Lori was a little heavier than Hannah, perhaps because she didn't keep up the same exercise regimen, but she was still attractive and dressed well. When you saw them together, you could easily tell they were sisters with similar classic features and blonde hair. John was still a partner in his law practice but had only been acting in an executive role remotely for the past few years. He appeared distinguished but was losing his hair and looking older since we last saw him. They had one daughter, Olivia, who was a senior in college.

Later, John cooked steaks on the outdoor grill, and Lori served a salad and baked potatoes paired with a bottle of Cabernet. After dinner, we just sat around, catching up over a second bottle of wine. John told us about their plan to take us out on the boat tomorrow.

"We can ride around the canals, then up the ICW. If it's not too rough, we can head out in the ocean and return that way."

By ten o'clock, we were exhausted and maybe a little drunk. We all went to bed, anticipating a great month ahead.

We had a full breakfast of bacon, eggs, and toast in the morning. Lori packed us a picnic basket with chicken salad sandwiches, fresh fruit, a bottle of rosé, and a variety of canned beverages. We wandered down to the boat dock, enjoying the beautiful weather and looking forward to our day. John started the engines, and we shoved off. We proceeded to putt around the canals in their neighborhood, admiring the homes. It was apparent that some were older, while others appeared to be brand new. And huge! Lori explained that builders were coming into these canal-front neighborhoods, tearing down the older existing houses and building these McMansions.

As she spoke, we worked our way north, exploring the finger canals and occasionally stopping if John thought something was worth seeing. By midday, we were nearing Pompano, and John found us a lovely little bay to drop anchor for lunch. The ladies placed the food from the basket on a folding table, and we all enjoyed the overstuffed sandwiches and fresh fruit. Hannah and Lori drank rosé, and John and I each had a beer. Other boats were doing the same thing in that little bay. Over time, the crowd grew, and we had front-row seats to great people-watching. Some could anchor like pros, and others had no idea what they were doing. A "cigarette" boat came in with three guys to tour the little bay, making a lot of noise. I find it comical that the advertisements for these boats always feature one guy with three hot girls in bikinis lounging on the bow, yet it's usually just guys I see on these boats.

After a couple of hours, John said, "Let's go up to the Hillsboro inlet and see how the ocean looks."

He fired up the engines while I pulled in the anchor. We headed up the ICW about a half mile, and John followed the buoys through the inlet. The current was going with us, and we were in the open ocean in a minute. John stated, "This is perfect. Maybe one-to two-foot waves."

We stowed anything that could fly around, and he opened it up, heading south. We were flying. He announced that we were doing fifty knots. It seemed much faster on the water through the waves than it would in a car. As we sped along, John asked, "Would you like to take the wheel, Bob?"

"Absolutely!"

The boat handled the seas beautifully. It was evident that it was built for speed in the open ocean. We went another five miles, and John pointed to a red buoy. "Go just to the left of that buoy, then we can turn into the Port Everglades inlet."

He slowed us down to 25 knots before directing me where to steer. When we got to the breakwaters, he took over the wheel and slowed it down to a no-wake speed.

"Hey, would you all like to stop at the 15th Street Fish House?" John asked the group. "We could have a drink and maybe stay for dinner."

"Great idea, John, I'd love to. Are you two are up for it?" Lori asked, looking at us.

"Sounds good to us," Hannah and I answered in unison.

John eased us onto the dock, and I helped him with the lines and fenders. He re-tied all my knots because I had no idea what I was doing. "I'll teach you a few knots next time we go out," he told me. "You only need to know three."

We went into the bar and ordered drinks. We talked and laughed and were enjoying ourselves. After an hour, we asked to be moved to a table and ordered dinner. Each of us ordered a different dish, and we shared them, along with another bottle of wine.

As it was beginning to get dark outside, we paid the tab and headed out to the boat. John got everything up and running with the lights on. We made our way up through the canals and were at their dock in no time. We tied up, stowed everything, and carried the empty basket to their house. Lori put on a pot of decaf, and we returned to the patio with our coffee and the brownies she had made earlier.

"What a wonderful day, you guys," Hannah said. "Truly delightful."

When Hannah and I got up in the morning, we wandered out to the kitchen to find a note from Lori. *I went to the grocery, and John is playing golf. I left coffee, juice, and croissants out for you. I'll be back before noon.*

We took our coffee out to the patio, enjoying the view once again. "Wouldn't it be nice to have a place like this for the winter?" asked Hannah.

"It sure would, but we'd have to sell the house in Westchester to afford something like this," I replied.

"We could never do that. I couldn't imagine not being around the kids and our friends for the whole year. Plus, I hear the summers are pretty brutal down here."

"I get that. Let me do a little research and see what we can afford."

"Well, while you do that, I'm going to put on a bathing suit and work on my tan."

While she was inside, I opened my iPad and started a real estate search. Hannah walked back out wearing a white one-piece I hadn't seen before.

"Is that new?" I asked. "I like it."

"Yes, I just bought it for the trip."

Seeing her in a bathing suit got my attention. At sixty years old and after having two kids, my wife still looked good.

She lay down on a lounger by the pool. "Do you need some help with the lotion?" I asked.

"Easy, big boy. Lori will be back any time now."

I busied myself on the iPad, looking at real estate listings in the area. I started by looking at properties up to $500,000. It appeared that anything close to the water would be a condo. I asked Hannah, "What would you think about a condominium?"

"Would it be near the water?" she asked.

"Yes, that's one of the filters I plugged in. A condo would be easier to close up for the summer, and all the maintenance would be handled. Plus, we could rent it out if we want."

"Let's go for a look."

"I'll pick out a couple close by, and maybe we can drive by this afternoon." I made a few notes of properties for us to see, and then we heard Lori coming out to the patio.

"I see you two made yourselves at home," she said. "I was hoping you would." She sat down on a lounger near her sister.

Hannah told her, "Bob and I were just discussing looking at a place for ourselves down here. Nothing like this, of course, but maybe a condo to spend the winters."

"I love it. You would be what we call snowbirds."

We sat around chatting with Lori about different areas we should look at. She had some suggestions for us. I told her about the places I found on the internet listings, and she agreed to drive us by them after lunch. She didn't think John would be home until two or three. Lori laid out freshly baked bread from Publix, deli roast beef, and potato salad. We ate outside, relaxing and enjoying the day while sipping iced tea. After lunch, Hannah helped Lori clean up and return everything to the kitchen.

"I'm going to change out of this suit, and then we can go," Hannah said. After a few minutes, both ladies were ready, and we got into the Highlander for the tour. The first place on my list was the Sea Colony. It was right on the Atlantic Ocean. It was a mid-rise condominium that looked old and run down.

"This looks pretty tired," Hannah noted.

"I have heard that it is," Lori agreed.

The next place we drove by was the Commander. It was a high-rise on the ICW in a very commercial area.

"I'm not sure I like this area," Hannah exclaimed. "But it does look a little newer."

In my thirty years of selling real estate, this is exactly how the initial phase of looking always goes. Everyone has to dis-cover what is available in their price range, then rule out some things and discover what is important to them. While returning to her house, Lori drove us by some other areas she thought we might like.

"I think I'll call the office and see if they might have a good referral agent for us down here," I said as we pulled into the driveway.

When we got back to Lori's house, I made the call. My office told me they would contact someone here and have them call me. I saw that the ladies were back out on the patio with John. I walked out and could hear them sharing our idea with him.

"Good to hear, old chap," he joked, attempting a British accent. "Would anyone like a margarita?"

He got a favorable response from all of us. As we were sipping our drinks, my phone rang. I could see it was from a local number, and I rose to take the call inside. She introduced herself as Marie Michaels and told me about receiving the referral call. I told her what we thought we were looking for and our budget. Marie said she would happily show us some properties she thought might fit the bill. We made an appointment for the following morning at ten. She offered to come pick us up and do the driving. I went back outside and told everyone our plans for tomorrow.

"Can I refresh your drink?" John asked.

"For sure," I replied, attempting a valley girl accent.

After a great meal with more wine, we all went to bed.

During breakfast with Lori and John, the conversation focused on our plans to look for a condo. Marie arrived right on time, and off we went in her Lincoln SUV. Marie was about our age, and I could tell she had been in the biz for a long time. She had what Hannah would call "big hair" and long manicured nails. She obviously spent time at the beauty parlor. I don't hold any of that against her. She was just a stereotypical real estate pro. We got to know each other a bit, and she asked us how far from Fort Lauderdale we would consider.

Hannah spoke up, "We're not really sure. Maybe up to an hour's drive, so long as it's near the water."

That was pretty much my feeling as well. "We'll be what you call snowbirds, so we don't want to be too far from an air-port," I added.

Marie replied, "Well, that doesn't put many limits on us. That means from Miami all the way up to Del Ray."

"I guess that sounds about right. So long as we can see the water."

Marie told us about the first place she was going to show us. It was a twenty-year-old two-bedroom condo in a three-story building just west of town on the New River. We noticed it was an attractive modern building with a gated entrance as we approached. We parked and went into the lobby. We rode the elevator to the second floor and walked down an exterior sidewalk to unit 202. Marie opened up and let us enter first. She turned on the lights and suggested, "You two look around while I open the storm shutters."

She opened the sliding glass doors and went onto the patio while we entered the kitchen.

"This is nice," Hannah said. "I'm not sure I love the countertops or the black appliances, though."

I agreed. "Each place we see will have a time stamp of what was trending when it was built. Unless it has been remodeled," I added.

After Marie opened the shutters, the rooms were flooded with light. We rushed to the patio to check out the view. We could see the boat docks on the river, and Marie explained that we could keep a boat up to fifty feet at the pier for a seasonal fee. I had been thinking about getting a sailboat someday, and I could see other good-sized sailboats at the dock, so I knew the depth was good. We continued our tour of all the rooms and naturally ended up back on the patio.

Hannah asked, "What do you think of the view from here, Bob?"

I focused on the view beyond the dock and said, "Well, we can keep an eye on the docks, but beyond that, I find nothing appealing."

Hannah agreed. "I don't see myself sitting out here with a glass of wine looking at the view."

"Okay, let's move on. You two look around and note what you like and don't like while I close up."

When we returned to the car, Marie said, "So a view from a patio or deck is important for you guys?"

Hannah replied, "Well, I guess it is. I didn't think it was a must-have, but now I can see it is."

Hannah and I commented about our initial impressions aloud while Marie drove us to the next place. We knew she would be listening intently to help her narrow the search.

The next place was in Hollywood. It was a high-rise that Marie told us was only fifteen years old and was right on the beach. Marie said it was a little over our budget, but we should look anyway.

As we approached, we could see the area was mostly newer high rises. Again, we had to enter a gate that opened after Marie entered a code. The lobby was gorgeous. The floors were all marble, and the space was decorated with fancy yet tasteful woodwork. Marie told us the listing agent was supposed to have opened the storm shutters earlier as we rode up the elevator to the ninth floor. Marie opened the door and again let us in first. We could immediately see out to the ocean through the sliding glass doors. Hannah went directly to the doors, opened them, and stepped onto the patio.

"Oh my!" she exclaimed. "This is fantastic."

I could tell from her body language that she was thrilled as we stood there, taking it all in.

"I thought you would like it," Marie declared.

"All right, how much?" I asked.

Marie replied, "They are asking $649,000, fully furnished. They paid a million for it in 2007."

I gulped but didn't fault her for showing us something over our budget. I knew she was just trying to show us what was out there and to educate us on values. Hannah and I continued our tour. Three bedrooms, two-and-a-half baths, 1400 square feet, all tastefully decorated and move-in ready.

"Is there any way we can afford this?" Hannah whispered in my ear.

"I don't see how," I replied softly, "unless we take out a mortgage."

"I have one more place to show you today," Marie said. "It's on the way back to where you're staying, and I promise it is within your budget."

We returned to her car and headed north. After crossing a drawbridge, we approached another high-rise. This one appeared older but looked well-kept. We could see a row of garages on one side of the parking lot.

"Do these units come with garages?" I asked.

"They are available for purchase, but the unit we are looking at does not come with one. If you are interested, I can find out the going price."

We entered the lobby, and Hannah said, "This isn't bad. It must have been updated at some point."

So, up the elevator, we went, this time to the fifth floor. Marie used a key to open the door, and we walked in. Once again, we looked at the kitchen while she opened the storm shutters. It smelled a little stuffy or moldy, but I thought maybe that was because it had been closed up for a while. The kitchen had been remodeled at some point, but it looked cheaply done.

Hannah pointed. "Look, there are popcorn ceilings throughout."

"And carpet," I added.

We checked out the two bedrooms and baths, then joined Marie on the patio. There was a nice eastward-looking view over the ICW. Similar to Lori and John's view but from much higher.

"How much is this one?" I asked.

"The asking price is $459,000," she replied.

"This one needs practically a whole gut job. It would be well over $500,000 by the time we finish."

"You can always make an offer below asking. It's been on the market for a while."

She asked, "How do you like the view, Hannah?"

"It's nice," she replied, "but nothing like the last one. I just loved looking out over the Atlantic."

As we headed out, Marie said, "I think I am getting a feel for what you guys are looking for. Can you give me a day or two to do some more research?"

"Certainly," I replied, "I think our heads are swimming right now."

We made an appointment for two days later. As she drove us back to Lori and John's, we asked her about restaurants she liked in the area. Hannah and I had been thinking of taking Lori and John out to dinner that night. She gave us a few suggestions, and we said our goodbyes.

We sat out on Lori and John's patio and wound down with drinks—white wine for the ladies and beer for John and me. We told them about what we had seen today and discussed the pros and cons of each property. "I've noticed that we always sit outside down here. I guess that will be an important factor in choosing a property," I said.

"That's for sure. We practically live out here, except in the summer."

We invited them for dinner at Anthony's, a place Marie had told us about. The food was good old-world Italian, and our discussion ranged from anything to everything. John asked how my golf game was.

"I haven't played in fifteen years, but I still have my clubs," I said.

"Do you want to go to the club tomorrow and hit some balls at the range? We could grab some lunch there," John offered.

"Sounds good to me," I replied, wondering if I really wanted to renew my love-hate relationship with that game.

"Oh good," Lori chimed in. "That will give Hannah and me a chance to do some shopping."

The following afternoon, after we had all returned from our separate ventures, I received a call from Marie. "What would you guys think about looking at an oceanfront building in North Miami Beach?"

I told her we would certainly take a look.

"Great. There is a place with two units available that I think you might like."

"Sounds good. Shall we say about ten o'clock?"

"Cool, I'll pick you up then," she replied.

The following morning, Marie arrived right on time.

"Good morning, Marie," we both said as we climbed into her car.

"Good morning. I'm glad you're willing to consider northern Miami Beach. I heard about a listing that just came on the market. While I was researching the recent sales data, I discovered another unit in the building that is available as well."

It was about a forty-minute drive from Lori and John's house. We went over a bridge onto the island and immediately noticed we were in an area of upscale high-rises. Marie gave us a little history of the area. "They started building here about forty years ago. The condos were mostly built in the eighties, but some are less than ten years old. The building we will be looking at is called Oceanside. It was built in 1981."

We entered an underground parking garage right off Collins Avenue. After exiting the car, Marie said, "Let's go to the lobby first. I'd like you to see it along with the main entrance and the pool area."

We rode a classy-looking elevator up to the first floor. When the doors opened, we could tell everything had recently been redone. There were marble floors and white painted panels on the walls. Each panel contained a piece of artwork. I was sure this was different from how it was decorated in 1981. She walked us out the front door under a portico where cars could pull up to drop off passengers. She then led us back to the pool deck overlooking the ocean with a grassy lawn between. Looking back at the building, we could see a social room on one side and a gym on the other. Some people were lounging by the pool, and one couple was relaxing in the Jacuzzi; everyone appeared quite happy. I noticed that the entire pool deck area needed to be updated to match the rest of the main floor. I guess in a building that's forty years old; it was all a matter of budget as to what got remodeled and when. I asked Hannah what she thought.

"So far, so good," she replied.

As we headed back in, Marie showed us the amenities and an area in the social room where yoga classes were held two days each week. I saw Hannah's eyes light up. Yoga was her current exercise of choice.

We returned to the elevator, and Marie told us, "There are two towers in this complex. Both of the units I will be showing you are in the east tower. Let's start with unit 505, the new listing."

We got off the elevator on the fifth floor and went down the walkway to the unit. Marie opened the door, once again letting us enter first. Immediately, Hannah went right for the patio. The view was spectacular.

"Oh, Bob!" she exclaimed. "This looks just like the other one that I liked."

"Okay, Marie, how much is this one?" I asked.

"They are asking $475,000."

Well, that's in the ballpark, I thought. Hannah and I inspected the unit more closely, pointing out things we liked and didn't like.

After a few minutes, Marie read from the notes on the listing. "It says here the unit is 1,025 square feet. The kitchen was redone in 2011, along with the ceilings and tile floors. It also says the sliders were replaced at that time, along with the AC unit."

"Wow. That's most of the big stuff," I said, impressed.

"What do you think of the grasscloth on the entry walls, Bob?" Hannah asked.

"I hate it. Along with some of the paint colors."

"I'm not sure I like the white appliances either."

"Honey, that's all easy stuff we can change ourselves," I assured.

She nodded and said, "We have done it all before. Are you still up to it? Remember, we're a bit older now."

"Oh, I remember every day, but I think so. Maybe we could hire someone to do anything that requires working on our knees."

We poked around for a few more minutes, and Marie asked, "Are you ready to see the other unit?"

"Sure," I replied. "Let's go."

The other unit was on the tenth floor. Marie unlocked the door and followed us in.

"Sort of smells like a wet dog in here," Hannah exclaimed.

"That's probably from the carpeting," Marie said. "Easy to change."

Instinctively, we gravitated to the patio and the view of the ocean.

"I do love the ocean," Hannah said. "I feel a little removed from the beach being up this high, though."

"I see what you mean," I replied. "Let's check out the rest."

We walked through the living and dining area, remarking at the mirrors covering one entire wall. We entered the kitchen. "This looks all original," I said. "Look at this ceiling. This all has to go."

Marie agreed, "Yes, it does look all original. That is what they called a dome ceiling back then. It was all the rage."

We continued looking around, noting what we would have to change.

Marie told us, "The listing says the AC unit was replaced in 2007 along with the water heater. The sliders look original to me."

I took out my phone to use the calculator. After about two minutes, I said, "We could easily put a hundred grand in this place. That's not counting all the things we haven't discovered yet. What are they asking for this place, Marie?"

"$450,000," she replied.

"What do you think?" I asked Hannah.

"I certainly like the other one better. I can see the light at the end of the tunnel there. I also prefer the view of the beach from that one."

"I agree. This one will need $100,000 right off the bat. The other one will cost about $25,000 to make it the way we want. And we can do that over time. What do you think, Marie?" I asked.

"Sounds like a no-brainer," she replied.

"Can we go back down for another look?" Hannah asked.

"Certainly," Marie said.

We went down and walked through again, inspecting everything more closely. From the foyer, the kitchen was on the left; then, you looked right through the open dining and living areas to the patio and the ocean. The bedrooms and baths were on the right. We all went out and sat on the patio and admired the ocean.

"I just love it," Hannah said excitedly. "What do you think, honey?"

"I agree. Marie, what should we offer?"

"Well, this one just came on for $475,000. The other one is on for $450,000. The recent sales are from $450,000 to $500,000 for these two-bedroom units. The three-bedroom and penthouse units are up to one million. I think it's worth the asking price, but we can start lower. What are your terms?" She paused before adding, "Any mortgage contingency?"

"No," I replied, "a cash offer with a quick closing."

"Then I suggest you go in at $450,000 and see where they come back."

I put my arms around Hannah and exclaimed, "Let's do it!" I could feel Hannah's excitement reverberating through me.

On the way back in the car, Marie told me she would try to put the offer in this afternoon and get back to us as soon as she heard anything. She gave us a copy of the listing and highlighted the common charges and taxes.

When we walked back into the house, Hannah went to find Lori, who was in her bathing suit by the pool with John. "We put in an offer!" Hannah announced.

"Fantastic. Tell me, tell me!" Lori said with excitement, giving her sister a big hug. "Wait, let me make us some drinks, and you can tell us all about it."

"I'm going to put on my suit. Be right back," Hannah declared.

So there we were again, out on the patio, sipping cocktails. This time, though, we were filling Lori and John in on the details of our new adventure. Hannah could not stop talking about the view. Lori and John were very excited for us and wanted to see it soon. I told them we would bring them with us if we came to terms with the seller.

During dinner, John asked if I was ready for a round of golf at his club.

"Sure, just don't expect too much from me."

We both laughed. I was starting to think we would love it down here, especially after hearing that snow was predicted in the forecast for the entirety of the northeast tomorrow. After dinner, my phone rang. I could see who it was from the caller ID. "Hello, Marie," I answered.

"Good evening, Bob. Is this a good time?"

"Sure."

"I think this is good news. I just heard from the listing agent. They countered at $460,000. There was a special assessment of $20,000 a couple of years ago, with $5,000 still due, but the sellers said they would cover that at the closing. What do you think?"

"Let me ask a little more about this special assessment. What was it for?"

"I am told this current one was for the elevator modern-izations and redecorating the lobby and social rooms," Marie explained. "There were also some minor concrete repairs included in that."

"How often can we expect special assessments?" I asked.

"In my experience, with a building this age, it can be once every five or ten years. Usually, they amount to a few thousand dollars to cover things that weren't in the reserve budget. But don't take my word for it. If you accept this counteroffer, we can add a contingency for a building inspection and a reserve budget review."

"Okay. We'll agree to the price of $460,000 with the contingency as you stated. Can we close within thirty days?"

"I have that date in the offer already. They shouldn't have a problem with the contingency; it's pretty common. I'll confirm that with you tomorrow morning, but I think you just bought yourself a beachfront condo!"

"Hannah will be thrilled. Goodnight, Marie."

"Congratulations, Bob," she replied.

I went back outside and told everyone the news. Hannah put her arms around me and gave me a big kiss. "Lori, you'll have to help us shop for furniture," she said, giddy with enthusiasm.

"You know I love shopping with you," Lori replied.

After sitting around for another hour, imagining our new future, we all turned in. Hannah invited me to join her in the shower, which I knew was an invite for romance. After drying off, we climbed into bed and made love to celebrate the new chapter in our lives.

Since we had no plans for the day, we slept until nine. We wandered out to the kitchen, poured ourselves coffee, and took it outside, where Lori was already sunbathing.

"No plans today," she said. "I'm just going to have a lazy day by the pool."

"Sounds good to me," Hannah said. "I'll put my suit on after I finish my coffee."

So that was how the morning went. John was at his golf club again. Around eleven, Marie called and said the deal was all set. She asked if she could come by for us to sign the papers in a little while. I asked the ladies if that worked for them.

"Ask her if we could meet at the condo later this afternoon," Hannah suggested. "I'd like to bring Lori with us to see it."

I relayed the question.

"Sure, we can do that," Marie agreed. "Shall we say three o'clock?"

I confirmed the time with the ladies, told Marie that was fine, and hung up.

"I'll text John to see if he wants to join us," Lori said.

We finished off the roast beef with iced tea and fresh-squeezed lemon for lunch and lounged around the pool until we heard the garage door open around two o'clock. "That would be John," Lori said. "He's going to join us. We need to get ready to leave in about fifteen minutes."

This time, John drove us in the Mercedes. It was just a few exits down Route 95, where the road split off for Miami Beach. The traffic got heavy, so it took us another twenty minutes to get out to the beach. We parked again in the underground garage and went up the elevator to the lobby, where Marie awaited us. She introduced us to Sandy, the property manager, who was very welcoming. I guessed Sandy was fifty-ish, with short blonde hair and bright blue eyes. We then rode the elevator up to the fifth floor, where Marie opened the door to 505. Hannah took Lori out to the patio and said, "Isn't this fantastic?"

Lori agreed. "I can see now why you like it. It's wonderful." Hannah then told her about the changes she wanted to make.

Marie set out the contracts on the kitchen counter for me to review. She explained that a title company would do the closing, although we could consult an attorney if we wanted. This differed from New York or New England, where attorneys did all the closings. As I searched through my pockets for my readers, Hannah teased, "Bob, I'm going to glue those things to your nose."

Hannah and I signed the papers, and Marie asked if we wanted her to schedule the building inspection.

"Sure," I said. "Can you arrange for the reserve review as well?"

"Absolutely," Marie answered. "I'll set it up ASAP."

"Perfect. Thanks so much for meeting us down here today."

"No problem," Marie replied.

We spent another few minutes walking around, discussing decorating ideas, and I made a list of things that needed to be done. We all said goodbye to Marie and thanked her again for meeting us at the condo. As Marie walked away, I realized how lucky we were to have found her. Throughout my life, there were only a few people I had met who were exceptional at their jobs. She was one of them; she was professional, efficient, honest, and enthusiastic about her work. Those were the traits of all the people who I felt were exceptional.

On the drive back, we continued to share our ideas about redecorating the unit. Our anticipation was growing. By then, the rush hour traffic had built, and the ride back took us over an hour. When we arrived, we sat by the pool, and I started looking at architectural websites on my iPad for decorating ideas. When I saw something I liked, I shared it with Hannah. On the Houzz website, there were thousands of pictures of recently completed work—bathrooms, kitchens, bedrooms—everything showing details of tile, paint colors, and decorating. It was a great way to see a completed design, imagine it in your space, and how to create it.

On the *Southern Living* website, there was a spread of pictures of a living room showing white shiplap on the lower half of the walls. The upper half was painted a medium gray. Hannah and I liked the look, and Lori liked it as well. We thought we could run it from the entry all the way through the living and dining area.

As we anticipated all this coming together, Hannah and I were getting excited about our new life in Florida. Well, at least our new winter lives. No more bundling up for the cold or standing by a window watching sleet and freezing rain. Winters in the north could be pretty harsh.

John grilled burgers, and the ladies continued to discuss decorating. After dinner, John and I went inside the house to watch an NFL playoff game.

We continued formulating our ideas and locating the materials for the next week or so. We decided to completely redo the hall bath immediately. We started searching for tile, and when we found some we liked, the store hooked us up with a contractor. Everything was coming together. Lori offered us the Jaguar to use any time we wanted. It was lovely driving a sports car around in the warm weather with the top down. At the end of the week, we met with the home inspector that Marie had arranged. He walked us through the unit, checking electrical outlets and looking inside the cabinets at the plumbing. He checked the operation of the windows and all the appliances and confirmed that the AC unit and water heater were relatively new. Everything seemed to be in order, but he did point out some breakers that needed updating. He assured me that he would include these details in his written report so we could negotiate with the sellers to cover the cost of replacing them.

His inspection was limited to our unit, and he explained that a structural review of the building was beyond his expertise. Such an assessment would be pretty expensive and require an engineer, but he did say that he stopped at the building department on his way this morning, and there were no outstanding issues or open complaints on file with their office.

On our way out, we stopped at the property manager's office, and Sandy gave us a copy of the current reserve statement, broken down into categories with amounts listed for each one. The total reserve account showed a balance of just over a million dollars in cash in various bank accounts. While that sounded sufficient, Marie advised that I review the statement with the title company or an attorney before the closing.

She excused herself for another appointment, and Hannah and I walked out to the pool area to look around. We must have appeared to be potential buyers because of how we dressed. A gentleman named Bob Randazzo introduced himself to us as a retired telemarketer from New York. I told him we were also from New York and that my name, also, was Bob.

He laughed and said, "Half the guys here are named Bob. It will take some getting used to." Although he was quite talkative and friendly, there seemed to be something a bit off about him. I couldn't quite put my finger on it.

We continued our exploration and walked down to the beach. "Can you just imagine, honey?" Hannah said. "We can do this every day."

We walked back through the lobby and asked Sandy if there was a local restaurant she would recommend.

"There's an Asian fusion place two blocks south," she replied. "They also serve fresh sushi. Lots of our residents go there."

We thanked her for the recommendation, walked out the front door, and headed south. After a bit, Hannah claimed, "I see a sign for Thai Basil. That must be the place."

We went in, and each ordered a different roll. When fresh, sushi was one of our favorites. It was, and we shared our rolls along with a couple of Kirin beers. After lunch, we explored the neighborhood while wandering back to the car. On our drive home, Hannah asked me what I thought of the home inspection.

"It seems everything is in order. I'm not surprised that he doesn't do a structural building inspection for just four hundred dollars. I'll review it with the title company along with the reserve account next week when we meet." I continued, "I don't see the point of hiring an attorney when the title company is doing the closing anyway."

Over the next few weeks, we drove around looking at furnishings, lighting fixtures, etc. Hannah and Lori found some lovely leather sofas at Macy's. We found a rug and some other things at HomeGoods. We swapped the Jag for the Highlander with Lori when we needed to bring something large back to their house. They were very accommodating, made us space in their garage to stash our stuff, and insisted that we stay until our unit was ready. They were going on a cruise the first week of February but said we should make ourselves at home—as if we already hadn't!

A few days before closing, the title company called and reviewed the closing statement numbers with us, and I wired the funds to them from our bank in New York. The closing was held at the title company office. Marie was there, but we never did meet the sellers. Over the next week, the tile contractor demoed the hall bath. He trashed everything except the bathtub itself. Then he re-tiled the whole room, replaced the vanity, and installed a new toilet. I had the materials and tools I needed to do the shiplap delivered from Lowes. It took me most of the week to complete it, and we hired a painter to come in and paint pretty much the whole place. We were now ready for furniture and to start sleeping there. *Hallelujah!* It was February 20, 2018. We were amazed that we could accomplish so much in just over six weeks from the time we stepped foot in the state of Florida.

I found us a reasonably priced rental car on a monthly basis. It was a small Honda SUV that was a few years old and would serve our purpose for $450 a month. Next year, we planned to buy a car that would stay in Florida all year.

On the last Saturday of the month, we attended the annual owners meeting with the board of directors in the social room, a large room just off the lobby. A kitchen area was open to the room at one end, with comfortable furniture clusters throughout the rest. A table was set up at the far end for the meetings, and additional folding chairs were set up to accommodate every-one. The entire room appeared to have been updated recently. Sandy introduced us, along with a few other new owners. Every-one was welcoming, and we were feeling optimistic about our move. The board members reviewed the standard reading of the minutes from the last meeting and the treasurer's report. Then, the president, Dave Davis, introduced the two new board members: Tom and Mike. Everyone seemed to know them well.

After proceeding to new business, the meeting was opened for discussion.

What a shit show! Hannah and I were shocked. They were complaining about everything. There was a crack in the pool deck. Water in the parking garage. The cost of the common charges. Some people were getting heated, and Dave did his best to keep things in order. Sandy would try to answer questions as best she could, but this crowd was pretty hostile. After a while, the most serious issue seemed to be the condition of the pool deck and the water in the garage. Mike and Tom proposed hiring an engineer to assess these two significant issues.

"That will just cost us more money. We just finished paying off a twenty-thousand-dollar assessment," someone shouted. There was cheering in agreement with him.

Dave once again tried to regain control. "How about we look into the cost of an engineer's inspection, and we will discuss it again at next month's meeting?" he offered.

People seemed to calm down after that.

He continued, "If all agree, we will get three quotes for consideration. We don't need a formal motion just to get a price quote."

So, the meeting was adjourned with little in the way of accomplishment. On the way out, we ran into our fellow New

Yorker, Bob Randazzo, and asked him his thoughts on the repairs discussed.

"I have no idea if repairs are needed. This board of directors always wants to spend money on something. Some of us are on fixed incomes and can't afford more assessments."

Hannah and I went up to our unit for lunch and discussed the shit show we had just observed. This was the first time we felt uncomfortable about what we had gotten ourselves into at Oceanside.

After eating, we headed to the pool for a swim and some sun. Some people were still grumbling about the meeting. There seemed to be two camps. One wanted everything kept in tip-top shape, and the other didn't want to spend any more money. The leader of the latter group appeared to be Bob Randazzo.

I guess that's just how it is in community living. We weren't sure which side we came down on but were certain we needed the engineer's inspection to understand the problems and the price tag.

Over the next month, we just relaxed and enjoyed our new lifestyle. We visited the pool or the beach almost every day, relishing our time in the sun. I noticed our love life had become more engaging. We felt like we were on a honeymoon and were very attentive to one another.

We shopped for items for the condo and met with Lori and John for dinner just about every week. We also started to make friends with some of the other residents. The age group of the residents seemed pretty much all over the place. Some were in their eighties and had been here a long time. Others were younger families and used their place as a weekend beach house, and lived or worked elsewhere in Florida. Of course, there were a lot of recently retired snowbirds, like Hannah and I.

Once again, there was a board meeting on the last Saturday of the month.

We went through the usual procedures and then got into the engineer's inspection fees. They all had come in at around $3,500 plus or minus a few hundred. This covered an initial half-day inspection with a written general findings report and recommendations for further in-depth inspections they felt were necessary. The board chose the middle-priced quote because they had positive reviews.

A motion was made, along with a second. All of the board members were in favor, so the motion passed. The next item on the agenda was a pending lawsuit against Islandia, the new high-rise next door. This was the first time we had heard about it. Apparently, when they were drilling deep for the footings several years ago, everyone could feel vibrations and trembling in both towers. Our board had hired a law firm and sued Islandia for ten million dollars.

"Our lawyers have informed us that we may be getting an offer to settle soon," Dave stated.

In response, there were the usual mumblings in the room.

Dave continued, "We have no idea what the amount is, so we will just have to wait and see."

The rest of the meeting was fairly peaceful, and I left feeling that we were on the right path.

As Easter approached, we started to think about when we might head back to Westchester. We decided to wait until the weather there was nicer than it was here. I did meet John out at the golf course one day. We played eighteen holes, and I shot a ninety-six with a couple of Mulligans. Rusty as hell, but I'd done better than I had feared.

By mid-May, we were back in New York. We got right back into the swing of things at home. We got together with our kids and went to the grandkids' soccer and little league games. Some of our friends were jealous of us and our second home. Some wanted to hear all about it because they were thinking about doing the same thing soon when they retired.

Despite that momentary second thought, Hannah and I were thrilled that we purchased the condo at Oceanside. We loved how our renovations turned out. We wanted to make a few more improvements and were looking forward to going down the following winter.

We did not follow the board meetings at Oceanside. While we did get reports of the meetings, when it came to our place in Florida, it was pretty much out of sight, out of mind. We did hear that a board member was leaving, and there was a formal call for candidates. I gave it no consideration whatsoever.

By mid-October, when the leaves started to fall, we started thinking about flying back down.

FALL 2018

We flew back to Florida on Halloween and rented a car for a week at the airport. Knowing that the cost of a rental car for six months would add up quickly, my first order of business was to buy a car.

When we got to the condo, we immediately opened the storm shutters on the patio and soaked in the sound and smell of the ocean. We arranged the patio furniture, and Hannah wiped the dust off while I shook up a batch of Cosmopolitans.

"Cheers!" we both exclaimed. "This is the life!"

That night, after showering, we made love wonderfully slow and gentle. Recently, we have come to enjoy the intimacy of taking our time and prolonging the pleasure.

The following morning, Hannah went grocery shopping. We had only picked up cream for our morning coffee on our way from the airport the previous evening. While she was out, I hunted for a car online. The last car we purchased was a certified pre-owned

Audi sedan that I loved. We got a nice low-mileage car at a reasonable price that would have been tough to afford if it were new. Plus, the warranty was for four years or a hundred thousand miles. Better than a new one! With that in mind, I thought we would ideally want an SUV because we were still buying stuff for the condo, and this would be our only car in Florida. I ended up finding a certified pre-owned Audi SUV at the nearby dealer. When Hannah returned to the condo, I helped her with the groceries and then showed her the car pictures on my iPad.

She asked, "Do we really need something that expensive down here? I was picturing something more like a Honda or Toyota."

"This one is used, just like the Audi we bought in New York. Let's think about it for a few days," I said. "I'll continue searching online."

Hannah made sandwiches for us, and we ate out on the patio. "How about we go down to the beach this afternoon," she said. "Maybe we can go for a walk to get some exercise."

On our way out, we passed through the lobby and saw a notice posted for the next board meeting. It would be the fifteenth of November. A little earlier in the month than usual so as not to interfere with Thanksgiving. The agenda stated that they would be reviewing the structural engineer's report.

We enjoyed our day at the beach. We must have walked two miles down and two miles back. One of the things we discovered about the beach was how much it could change from week to week. If a storm had recently come through, there could be a shelf cut into the sand halfway up the beach, forming an upper and lower level. Within a few days, it would level itself out. On other days, there could be seaweed or debris on the beach, then that would wash away a few days later. Another thing we learned was how much easier it was to walk on hard sand near the water at low tide.

When we got back to our chairs, we sat and rested, sipping water and enjoying the sun on our skin. Jim, one of the residents we had met previously, stopped by to say hello. After the usual pleasantries, he asked if we had heard anything about the engineer's report. We told him we hadn't.

"I hear it is pretty serious. No numbers yet, but worse than we expected."

"I guess we'll find out at the meeting."

"That we will," he replied. "Enjoy your day," he added as he walked away.

"Good to see you," we hollered back before he got too far.

I told Hannah, "Maybe you're right—we should find a less expensive car. It sounds like the bills around here could be more than we planned on."

We spent our time at the beach or by the pool for the next week. Hannah had joined a yoga class and enjoyed it. "This is the best I've felt in weeks," she exclaimed.

We found a two-year-old Mazda CX5 nearby with low miles that came with the CPO warranty. After picking it up, we dropped the rental car off at the airport in Fort Lauderdale and met Lori and John for dinner since we were nearby.

The following Saturday, we went down to attend the meeting. We saw the board members all at the table upfront, along with Sandy. They looked pretty serious. After everyone had filed in, Dave called the meeting to order with the standard procedures. He then introduced Lindsay, our newest board member, who lived on the second floor in the south tower, overlooking the pool.

Dave announced, "Our first order of business is the engineer's report." There were some anxious murmurs from the crowd. He told us that copies of the report would be made available by Sandy for anyone who asked. He then went on to describe the engineer's findings.

"The first item in the report is that the whole pool deck is pitched incorrectly. It should be higher in the center and lower at the outside edges. He believes the deterioration and settling of the central columns at the garage level have caused this. The second item is the water in the garage. The improper pitch of the pool deck is the primary cause of this water problem. The third item of concern is the deterioration of the main support beams under the pool deck. Their structural integrity has been substantially compromised from the constant moisture caused by this same problem. These columns are made of steel-reinforced concrete. The steel rebar within the beams is rusting and eroding due to moisture and salt air from the ocean's proximity. Because of that, the concrete is also losing its strength and crumbling." Dave paused, then said, "I spent an hour with the engineer when he was here. I pressed him to give us an estimate for the repairs. He told me he could not do that, although his best guess was closer to ten million than five million."

The crowd erupted.

"We can't afford that. Are you nuts?" I heard from behind us.

"No way!" someone hollered. "We'll have to move."

"My brother is an engineer," Martha, from 202, said. "I want to get his opinion."

Dave let the chaos die down a bit. "Sure, Martha, we would be happy to get his opinion. Ask Sandy for a copy of the report, and you can send it to him."

The grumbling continued.

"We need a second opinion," suggested another person beside me.

"This will cost forty thousand dollars per unit," another homeowner claimed after crunching the numbers in his head.

When things quieted, Dave said, "Well, a second engineer's report will cost us another thirty-five hundred. Do we want to spend that?"

The comments and opinions continued. Hannah and I were wondering what we got ourselves into and questioned the wisdom of our purchase once again.

Dave asked, "Can I have a motion to table this discussion until the next meeting?"

From the board table, Tom announced, "I'll make that motion."

"I'll second it," Mike said.

"All in favor?" Dave asked.

The board passed the motion unanimously.

Dave continued, "We will consider where we go from here at the next meeting. To get an accurate estimate, we must hire the engineer to produce plans and a bid package to go out to contractors for quotes."

After a few more minutes, the meeting was adjourned. There was quite a buzz in the air as everyone filed out. This was the topic of discussion around the building for the rest of the week while people were making plans for Thanksgiving. Some were going back north to be with family. We decided to stay and spend the holiday with Lori and John.

As we passed through the lobby multiple times daily, we got to know and like Sandy. She was a reliable source of information. Due to the holidays, we discovered that the next meeting would be at the end of January. We flew back home to spend Christmas with our children and grandchildren. While we enjoyed the holiday with them, it was cold in New York, and we couldn't wait to return to Florida.

WINTER/SPRING 2019

We returned the first week of January to the beautiful weather in Florida. Once again, we enjoyed ourselves on the beach or at the pool while watching the weather up north on TV. We were sure that the meteorologists down here took joy in the suffering of people up north. Hannah had resumed her yoga classes, I played golf, and we took long walks on the beach together.

The end of the month signaled it was time for another board meeting. The meeting started with the usual procedures; then, we got to old business. There were many questions about the engineer's report. Martha told us that her engineer brother thought the problem was quite serious and needed to be addressed soon. Someone else had sent the report to an engineer friend, who agreed it needed to be repaired ASAP.

After more discussion, the board engaged the engineer to develop a repair plan. George, the treasurer, told us he would find the $25,000 for the engineer's fee elsewhere in the budget. The meeting continued onto other old business, then to new business. Some agenda items had to do with banking, then on to open discussion.

As we had learned, board meetings were mainly a bitch fest of people asking for repairs. Some people blamed mold in their unit on the management. One lady up front wanted to replace all the lounges by the pool. Hannah and I thought it was ridiculous to consider spending money until the structural repair was resolved. We could be facing millions of dollars in repairs, and it wouldn't be wise to spend whatever funds we had on lounge chairs. The meeting eventually adjourned, and we all went about our daily routines.

We were learning how crowded Florida could become during the winter months, otherwise known as snowbird season, and we were part of the problem. Getting a restaurant reservation anywhere was hard, and the traffic was brutal. But the weather was nice, so we all dealt with it. We skipped the next couple of board meetings because we knew the engineer's plan would not be completed yet, and quite honestly, it wasn't enjoyable to sit around and listen to people bitch.

We started thinking about when to return to New York when spring was upon us. By mid-May, when the temperature reached ninety-three degrees, we flew home. Once we returned to our suburban New York routine, we had our kids and grandkids to the house for Memorial Day. I asked my younger son, James, if he wanted to play golf sometime.

"I haven't played yet this year, but I would love to," he replied.

I told him I had been playing with Uncle John once a week in Florida. "Maybe I can finally beat you," I challenged.

We did play, and I beat him, but I could tell it would be the only time that would happen all year after he shook off the rust. I joined a senior league at Sprain Brook Golf Club and continued playing once a week.

Sandy updated us on the goings on at Oceanside with a monthly newsletter. We knew there was nothing that could be accomplished until the engineer's report came back. According to the newsletter, the engineer hoped to complete his work by early September. Hannah and I thought it seemed like a long time to wait for something this urgent. We learned the following month that it would be presented at the September meeting.

FALL 2019

We decided to go down early this year to attend the September meeting. We flew down a week after Labor Day, and even though it was hot, we found it quite enjoyable without the winter crowd. This month's meeting had fewer residents in attendance as most snowbirds had not yet arrived.

The meeting started in the usual fashion. Dave had laid out plans and drawings for us to see. I was surprised how many people thought they knew what they were looking at. Sandy stated that she would seek bids from three contractors as required in our condominium documents and that it could be a few weeks before they were all in. The meeting adjourned with little else of importance to discuss. Hannah and I were disappointed that nothing was accomplished at the meeting we had flown down early to attend.

Late September and October were lovely in southern Florida, so long as a hurricane didn't come through. Everyone was watching the weather forecast daily. Fortunately, we were lucky this year. The oppressive heat of the summer months had subsided, and we were enjoying our days on the beach. I resumed playing golf each week with John, and they invited us out on the boat a few times. We enjoyed our time with them, and Hannah appreciated reconnecting with her sister.

We gathered in the social room for the board meeting on the last Saturday of the month. George, our treasurer, reviewed our financial statement and announced that our reserve account had grown slightly over the previous year to $1.2 million.

The first item up in old business was the bids from the contractors for the engineer's plan for concrete repairs. Dave said, "I'll cut to the chase and give you the numbers first. We can discuss the variances in the bids later. The three bids came in at $8.9 million, $9.5 million, and $11.4 million." The sound of gasps filled the room. Hannah and I were surprised no one fainted.

Our treasurer, George, told us, "That breaks down to between thirty thousand and ninety-thousand per unit, depending on the documented formula. The three-bedroom penthouse units will be in the upper range, of course. On average, it will be around $47,500 per unit." Again, sounds of disbelief echoed throughout the room.

Bob Randazzo, the telemarketer, said, "That will mean a second mortgage for us."

"Yeah, we'll need to get a mortgage, too!" another homeowner exclaimed.

I spoke up and offered, "The good news is that our property values have increased a hundred thousand over the past year. You won't have much trouble getting a mortgage." Of course, I wasn't aware of everyone's financial condition.

Sandy announced, "We have secured a favorable rate from our bank for home equity loans. I have all the information for you in my office."

Dave Davis conceded, "We will not decide on this today. I would like to form a committee to review the bids and make a recommendation at the next meeting. Raise your hand if you would like to volunteer."

I looked at Hannah for approval. She nodded, and I raised my hand along with two other people.

"Thank you," Dave said. "The committee will be the three of you, myself, and another board member." He looked around the board table, and Mike volunteered.

"Thank you, Mike. Can I have a motion to form the bid review committee?" A motion was made, seconded, and passed unanimously.

Sandy added, "I'll speak to each of you to figure out a time to meet."

So, there you have it; I was now on a committee. The meeting wound down, and we all filed out. We stopped to speak with Jim McCarthy, whom we always saw on the beach, on the way out. He also had volunteered.

"Would you and Karen like to come by for cocktails this afternoon?"

"Let me check with her first, but it sounds good to me."

Sandy asked Jim and me when we would be available. We gave her some times, and she thanked us, explaining that she would get with Dave and pick one. Hannah and I went up for lunch, and Jim called me right back.

"Karen says she would love to. What can we bring?"

"We have pretty much everything except gin," I replied.

"That will work for us. Karen said she'll bring some snacks."

"Great, shall we say around four-thirty?"

"Perfect."

After lunch, we went down to the pool. There was always a lot of discussion after a board meeting. I suspect that some cliques were forming. From what we overheard, some people didn't want to spend money on anything, and some were afraid the building would fall down.

When Jim and Karen arrived, the drink consensus was Moscow Mules. I made four of them, and we all went out on the patio. We had only met them briefly a few times over the last year on the beach. Hannah and Karen had seen each other at yoga, so we told each other a little bit about ourselves, and as it turns out, we had quite a bit in common.

Jim was slightly older than me, with pure white hair and a full beard. Karen appeared a little younger and had dark hair that was naturally turning gray. They were both retired professionals from Michigan; they had come from previous marriages and met only a few years before becoming snowbirds. I asked them what their thoughts were on the structural work.

"Well, in my mind, it needs to be done," Jim said.

"It can't wait," Karen added. "We're wondering if it's even safe to live here."

"That's our feeling as well," Hannah agreed.

I jumped in. "It's good to find some like-minded people here. I'm not sure everyone here is on the same page."

"I know what you mean," Jim concurred. "We heard people whispering about impeaching the board."

"I'm not sure that's even something that can be done," I said.

"Well, I look forward to working with you on the committee," Jim replied. "I hope the rest of them are rational thinkers!"

We had another drink and decided to wander down to the Asian fusion restaurant for dinner. We all seemed to have fun; perhaps we might become good friends.

A few days later, at our first committee meeting, Dave welcomed us all. He stated that our goal was to choose one of the contractors based on what we felt was necessary. "Price is not the only factor here. We need to ensure they all understand the scope of work and are using the same materials."

Sandy had made copies of the bids for each of us. Mike had been a builder for most of his life and seemed to know the key elements to look for. As we studied the bids, we started to note some differences. Then, we pointed each factor out to each other and tried to determine its importance. Dave stated after a couple of hours, "I think that's enough for today. I can't focus my eyes anymore."

We all took our copies with us—we'd have some serious homework to do, and we made plans to meet at the same time next week. Throughout the week, I diligently reviewed the plans, making notes of the differences between each bid.

One day, while at the pool, I ran into Jim, and he mentioned that he was working on a spreadsheet to keep track of the differences.

By our next meeting, we had become pretty familiar with the bids and were able to ask more informed questions. One notable observation I made was that the quote from Blue Water Contractors was better organized and easier to follow. I wondered if their work would also reflect this level of professionalism. After I brought up that point, the others immediately agreed. As Jim walked us through his spreadsheet, the group was impressed—it helped us stay organized.

At the end of an hour, Dave asked, "Shall we take a vote?"

I started by stating, "My vote is Blue Water."

As we went around the table, the decision was unanimous—Blue Water, the median bid at $9.5 million.

"Let's all keep this decision under our hats until the next board meeting, please," Dave said.

We all agreed and headed out with a sigh of relief.

When I returned to our unit, Hannah asked, "How did it go?"

"Quite well. We all agreed on the same contractor."

"And who is that?" she asked.

"It is supposed to be a secret," I replied.

"That's okay. I can wait until the meeting," she smiled.

Over the next week, I played golf with John as usual. We now had a regular foursome. At one of our dinners with Jim and Karen, she casually inquired, "Does it seem like everyone's name is Bob around here?"

I laughed, "Whenever I hear someone say, 'Hi, Bob!' I think they're talking to me. I know I have a common name, but this is ridiculous!"

The November meeting occurred a week earlier than usual, on the Saturday before Thanksgiving. After addressing the initial matters, our president thanked all committee members for their service. He briefly discussed the differences in the bids and explained the reasons behind selecting Blue Water as the contractor. He explained that the price was set at $9.5 million, then turned the meeting over to George to lead a discussion on how we might finance the project. Sandy distributed worksheets that outlined various options applicable to each unit type.

George began by stating, "As you can see, the assessment for each unit will be from roughly thirty thousand for one-bedroom units on up to ninety thousand for three-bedroom penthouses. We can spread these payments over three installments within a year and a half, or the association can take out a five-year bank loan while increasing the common charges by $1800 to $4500 per quarter."

The room erupted with grumbling.

He continued, "Clearly, the bank loan will result in higher costs in the long run, but it does provide the advantage of spreading the payments out over a longer period." He paused to the sounds of discontent, then added, "In addition to the interest charges, the bank will require us to provide them with an engineer's report before releasing each installment of funds as they will oversee the entire project."

The floor was then opened for discussion and questions. Some people advocated for the three-payment plan because it left us in control of the project and was the most cost-effective in the long run. Others favored the bank loan plan to remove each resident's immediate financial burden. The discussion got pretty heated.

"Why can't we use the $1.2 million we have in the bank to put towards this?" Bob Randazzo asked.

"Good question," George noted and then went on to explain. "All that money is earmarked for specific reserve items as required by Florida condominium law. There is a whole list of categories for things like roofing, paving, or plumbing. There is only one hundred ten thousand in reserve for concrete repairs."

Someone else exclaimed, "How do you expect us to come up with fifty grand in a year?"

"That's ridiculous. Do you think we are all rich?" another voice shouted from the back of the room.

Many agreed with that position, and the heated exchange continued for another half hour.

"What you are proposing is unconscionable!" a lady yelled angrily.

George stood up to try to take control. He went on to show examples of using a home equity loan to help with the payments.

He asked if anyone had contacted the bank about this matter. Only one person claimed they had.

Dave stood up. "Thank you, George. I know it was a lot of work on your part to crunch all those numbers. Does everyone understand what we're up against?"

An older lady at the front of the room started to cry, prompting George to offer her assistance privately later.

"I think we should table this discussion until the next meeting," Dave interjected. "Hopefully, many of you will explore obtaining a home equity loan. Can I have a motion to adjourn?"

A motion was made and seconded, and the meeting was adjourned. As we filed out, a hushed silence fell over the room, and it seemed some people were in a state of shock. Upon reaching our unit, I was still wound up and decided to crack open a beer. "Would you like something?" I asked Hannah.

"A beer will be fine." She sounded defeated, and I assumed she felt as I did—disappointed at the lack of consensus among the owners and the unawareness of the urgency to start the work. Although it was just past noon, we sat at the table, sipping our beers, attempting to make sense of all the drama of the board meeting. Gradually, we calmed down, and Hannah took some leftovers from the fridge and served lunch. Hannah and I weren't overly distraught by the assessment. We certainly didn't want to fork over $50,000, but we could do so.

This situation was exactly what a rainy day fund was for—I just hoped it didn't keep raining!

The holidays were approaching again, and, as we had hoped, Lori and John invited us to their house for Thanksgiving. We were thrilled to learn that their daughter, Olivia, would join us after her summer abroad in Europe. Hannah was her godmother and hadn't seen Olivia for two years. She had graduated college this past spring, and it was a delightful day hearing all about Europe through Olivia's eyes.

We flew home for Christmas once again to be with our children and grandchildren. Luckily, it snowed on Christmas Eve, and we played in the snow with them all on Christmas Day. We even taught the grandkids how to build a snowman!

WINTER/SPRING 2020

It was now the beginning of the "season," and the building was filling up. Some days, securing a lounger by the pool was tough, especially when people would arrive as early as 7:00 in the morning and claim a chair with a towel or book! Something else to add to the bitch-fest at the next meeting, I thought.

We heard a rumor that Mike would not run for another term on the board. Sure enough, Sandy posted a notice a few days later calling for candidates for the upcoming election and a reminder that the next board meeting was scheduled for the following Saturday.

Later that week, we ran into Mike and his wife, Beth, walking the beach. We stopped to greet them, and I asked about the board. True to the rumors, he told us he would not serve another term.

"Things are just getting too crazy around here. Quite frankly, I'm concerned about being sued personally if something were to happen."

After they walked away, Hannah said, "Wow, I hadn't even thought of that."

"Neither had I."

After the preliminaries, we returned to the assessment discussion at the January meeting. George took the floor and asked how many of us had met with the bank to look into a home equity loan. One gentleman spoke up, "Yes, we did. We were considering taking one out to redo our kitchen anyway. Now, it will just need to be larger."

A few more people discussed their inquiries with banks and offered their opinions. George reiterated his train of thought. "We really would rather not have the bank running the show here, and I'm not sure we are comfortable with this association taking on that kind of debt."

Dave retook the floor and said, "Thank you, George. I would like to poll the membership. Can I have a show of hands of who favors the three-payment plan?" It appeared that over half of the people in the room raised their hands. "Now, how many of you prefer bank financing?" Dave asked.

There were substantially fewer hands raised. I guess that shows something about the financial position of our residents, I thought to myself. Hannah and I had discussed it, and we preferred the three-payment plan, but we would certainly understand if the vote went the other way. So long as the work got done.

Dave asked, "Can I have a motion to self-finance with the three-payment plan?" George made the motion. Lindsay seconded it. "All in favor?" Dave asked. Dave, George, Tom, Mike, and Lindsay raised their hands and said, "Aye."

"The Ayes have it, unanimously," announced Dave. "We will work with George and Sandy to produce a payment schedule for each of you in the next few weeks."

A whole lot of grumbling ensued. A few people shouted, "I can't pay that!"

Eventually, the room quieted down. Dave stood again and announced, "The next order of business is the Islandia lawsuit. Our attorneys informed us that we have an offer of one million dollars on the table; I'll remind you that our suit is for ten million."

Everyone seemed to have an opinion on the settlement offer.

"They'll go way more than that!" The room seemed to agree with that thought. Someone stood and asked if that money could offset the assessment.

"It certainly can," Dave said. "However, our attorneys recommend letting them negotiate a higher amount."

"There you go!" another person shouted.

Dave continued, "Whatever amount we settle for will go against the assessment. Do I have a motion to decline this offer and have the attorneys negotiate?"

The motion was made, seconded, and it carried unanimously. Dave remained standing and said, "Sandy tells me that no one has come forward yet in the call for candidates. I would like to remind everyone that this is an opportunity to shape the decisions around here at this most critical time. I hope some of you will consider serving a two-year term."

I felt some soul-searching among the owners, yet no one spoke up. There was no further business, so the meeting was adjourned in the usual fashion. On the way out, there were a few positive mumblings that the Islandia settlement could offset the assessments.

After another couple of days of "living the life," we heard a rumor that Sandy had given her two-week notice to resign. When Hannah went downstairs to get the mail the next day, she stopped by the office and asked Sandy if the rumors were true. Sandy explained that she could no longer take the anger that so many residents expressed to her. "I'm not a punching bag," she exclaimed. Now, the board had to search for a replacement for her, too.

Around this time, we started hearing on the news about a new virus from China called COVID-19. They thought it may have originated from bats or a laboratory. Initially, we weren't overly concerned; we had heard about similar outbreaks like

Sars and the Bird Flu occasionally over the last few years, and nothing had ever come of it.

Another week went by, and we all received our assessment payment notices. We would have to come up with $15,830 in sixty days. We had already done the math and had made plans to transfer the funds to our checking account.

A few days later, we heard a knock on our door. It was Bob Randazzo, the telemarketer from New York.

"Hi, Bob."

"Hi, Bob." He chuckled and asked if we had a moment.

"Sure. Come on in. Would you like a beer or a Diet Coke?"

"No, thanks. I'll only take a few minutes of your time."

He showed us a petition he had been carrying, explaining that many residents were protesting the assessment. I could see there were dozens of signatures already. He told us, "Not all the residents can afford the payments. Some will have to sell and move out."

I glanced at Hannah. "I'm sorry, but we won't sign the petition, Bob. I understand how tough the payments are, but the work has to be done, and we feel this is the best way to do it." Then, I added, "If some of them decide to sell, they will have made a substantial profit on their units. They should be able to find something they can afford."

Sounding disappointed yet understanding, he thanked us for our time and rose to leave.

"Hope to see you on the beach soon," Hannah said as he walked out.   "Wow," I said, turning to Hannah. "I'm glad I'm not on the board! They'll have their hands full with Sandy leaving and now this petition."

The following week, we all got a notice from the board informing us that they found a new property manager. They asked us to all welcome Diane, who would start on Monday.

Over the weekend, we went on the boat again with Lori and John. They had invited Jim and Karen to join us as well. We had introduced them to one another at a dinner party we held a few weeks ago. We came down the ICW past our condo and viewed Miami from the water. We then tied up at a marina and went to South Beach for lunch. Everyone had a great time, and Lori and John seemed to hit it off with Jim and Karen.

After returning to Fort Lauderdale in the boat, we were thoroughly exhausted from our day in the sun. We thanked them for a beautiful day, bid them a good evening, and rode back to Miami in our car.

Hannah and I stopped by the office on Monday to greet Diane and welcome her. We learned that she had previously managed a property in Miami proper and had experience with major construction projects. We chatted for a few minutes, then wandered out to the pool.

"She seems nice," Hannah observed.

"Yes, she does," I added, "I think her construction experience will be valuable around here over the next year or two."

At the next meeting on the last Saturday in February, Dave rose to address the room. Once the standard introductory remarks were out of the way, he informed us that the county would require us to undergo a forty-year recertification process over the next year, which needed to be completed by December 31, 2021. He stated, "We have reached out to the structural engineer who did our concrete plan, and he is willing to do it for five thousand dollars. Diane has checked around and found that this seems to be the going price for a building of our size."

The announcement was met with some grumbling.

Dave, still standing, stated, "We don't have any choice. It is required by law. Can I have a motion to hire our engineer to do this recertification?"

George made the motion; Tom seconded it; all four remaining board members said "Aye," and the motion carried.

"Okay, we can open the floor to the members for open discussion."

Bob Randazzo stood up and said, "May I address the board?"

"Sure, Bob. The floor is yours."

"I have a petition with sixty signatures requesting that we reconsider the structural repair payment plan."

There was applause from many in the room.

He went on to say, "I have invited the local building official here today to express his opinion of our building. I would like him to speak now if it is okay with the board."

I whispered to Hannah, "I didn't see this coming." She squeezed my hand.

The board members looked at each other, and then Dave Davis said, "Sure, go ahead."

He stood and introduced himself as Peter Tomasi, our local building inspector. "A few of the residents here approached me last week to ask if I would look at the building and tell them if I think this proposed work is needed. We walked the property yesterday, and they showed me the areas of concern along with a copy of the plan for repair from your engineer. While I agree that these repairs should be done at some point, I don't see a rush. Your building is in fine shape."

The room erupted. The board members huddled together with Diane. It didn't seem like they knew what to do next.

Dave stood and asked for quiet. He then addressed Peter Tomasi. "When do you think this work needs to be done?"

Mr. Tomasi replied, "I think within three to five years would be appropriate."

Again, the room erupted in chaos as everyone engaged in animated conversations with those beside them. Meanwhile, the board members huddled together, talking among themselves.

After a few minutes, Dave finally stood up again and stated, "Given this new opinion, we believe it would be best to table this discussion for now. We will convey Mr. Tomasi's opinion to our engineer and resume this conversation at a special meeting in two weeks. Can I have a motion to adjourn?"

We adjourned. However, many people remained in the room to question Mr. Tomasi. You would have thought he was Elvis!

Over the next week, we continued enjoying our time at the pool or on the beach. I joined John for our regular foursome, and Hannah took the yoga class with Karen. We overheard some people complaining about pieces of the patio deck above them falling. The next time we saw Diane, she asked us if we had any similar issues. We told her this was all news to us, but we had noticed a couple of pieces broken off from the edges of other decks. She said she was aware of that and asked us to let her know if we had any issues on our patio. We promised to keep her informed if we saw anything of concern.

Around that time, the news became increasingly focused on this new COVID-19 virus. The CDC suggested that wearing masks might become a necessary precaution for everyone. Hannah and I had continued our habit of watching the news every night during dinner. The number of people dying or being hospitalized was alarming. We saw images of hospitals running out of rooms, placing patients in the halls, and refrigerated trucks serving as temporary morgues. Senior citizens seemed to be the most likely to suffer, and the news crews were focused on the elderly living and nursing homes in southern Florida. Yet, our new president came on the TV telling us there was nothing to fear and that the virus would pass soon.

When Saturday rolled around, we all assembled again in the social room. Hannah turned to me and whispered, "I never imagined condo living could be so full of drama."

The special meeting commenced, the preliminaries were addressed, and Dave told us about their discussion with the engineer. "He informed us that he cannot predict exactly when the structure might fail. He also made clear that he disagreed with Mr. Tomasi's assertion that 'the building is in fine shape.'

He recommended that we begin the work as soon as we can afford to do so."

So there it was. The timing just changed from as soon as possible to as soon as we could afford it. Dave told us he had asked the engineer to come out and look at our patio decks, and then he opened the meeting to discussion.

Many people suggested that the structural project be delayed for one year so we could start raising money to put toward the work. That discussion lasted for another half hour when Dave called for a vote. "Can I have a motion to postpone the start of work for one year?"

George made the motion, and Tom seconded it.

"All those in favor?"

Dave and Lindsay raised their hands and said, "Aye."

"All those opposed?"

George and Tom raised their hands and said, "Nay."

So the vote was two to two. Since we were down to four board members, we were deadlocked. The board looked at each other, wondering what to do.

Dave announced, "Because of a tie vote, we'll need to table this until a fifth person is elected. If no one volunteers to run, we will have no choice but to appoint someone." He asked our property manager, "Is that the correct procedure, Diane?"

"Yes, it is, Dave. Unless one of you changes your vote."

"Anyone?" Dave asked, looking at each board member.

When no response came, he concluded, "Okay, can I have a motion to adjourn?"

We adjourned.

I whispered to Hannah on our way out, "This is getting more interesting by the day."

"That it is."

That evening, we were invited to Jim and Karen's for dinner. We went up to their unit on the ninth floor at 6:30. We discussed the morning's meeting over drinks.

"We are testing the bounds of community living," Jim remarked.

"That's for sure," I replied. "I'm glad Diane knows all the rules."

Jim added, "The pressure around here to join the board will intensify."

The drinks and discussion continued until Karen announced dinner. She had prepared steak au poivre, and it was delicious.

The following week, we all received a notice that one new candidate was willing to run for the board. Enclosed was his resume, along with his thoughts on directing our building. It was Bob Randazzo. "I guess we know how the vote will go now," I remarked to Hannah.

There was an additional notice that another meeting would be a week from Saturday.

"Do we really have to go?" Hannah asked.

"You don't," I replied. "One of us should be there, though. I'll go."

"Thanks, honey. I just can't take much more of this drama."

As the week went by, she made plans with Karen to go shopping on the day of the meeting, leaving Jim and me to attend on our own.

Bob Randazzo was introduced as our new fifth board member at the meeting.

They held the vote once again. It was a three-to-two vote in favor of delaying the start of the project for one year and revisiting the payment plan, just as we expected. Our president, Dave, informed us that the engineer had looked at the patio decks and would need to do a more thorough inspection before determining what needed to be done. The price for this inspection would be $4500. "Can I have a motion to engage the engineer?" he asked.

"I'll make that motion," Tom offered.

"I'll second it," said George.

"All in favor?"

Four hands went up with an "Aye."

"All those opposed?"

Bob Randazzo's hand with up and declared, "Nay."

"The motion carries."

Jim and I looked at each other and wondered if Bob Randazzo would oppose spending money on anything. Only time will tell.

Dave announced that he would propose that another committee be formed after the engineer had done his report on the patio decks. He then asked, "Diane, will you send out notices that the assessment has been suspended and ask members not to send in the payments?"

Diane agreed, and Dave adjourned the meeting with the usual procedure.

It was now the middle of March, and the gravity of the Covid virus situation was intensifying. Disturbing news reports revealed hospitals struggling to cope with an influx of sick people. Many people worldwide were dying because no one knew how to treat the virus. In response to the escalating crisis, the government issued mandates requiring everyone to wear masks in public, maintain a minimum of six feet from others, and practice diligent hygiene by thorough hand washing before and after touching anything. The grocery stores were running out of all paper and cleaning products. The hoarding had begun.

We were both trying to get a handle on the whole Covid thing. To be honest, we were scared and were taking it very seriously. We called our kids to make sure they were all right. We asked about our grandchildren; they told us they were not allowing them to attend school.

By the end of March, people were instructed to refrain from going to their workplaces whenever possible, instead working remotely from home. Restaurants and bars were forced to shutter their doors. All the schools and daycare centers were closed, forcing parents to stay home.

It was becoming impossible to buy masks or hand sanitizer, and some people began to make cloth masks at home—at least those who could sew. Hannah was able to make masks, and she passed them out to people in the building. Then, before we knew it, the health department recommended that we close our pools, and the March and April board meetings were canceled.

We weren't supposed to drive a car unless it was to the grocery or drug store or if someone was considered a "critical worker." The only silver lining we encountered was that road traffic was down to nothing, and gas prices had fallen dramatically. First, the airlines stopped flying, then re-opened, not allowing anyone to sit in a middle seat. They claimed to sanitize the whole interior of the planes between flights.

After a month of this unprecedented situation, the economy had fallen off a cliff—as you can imagine. Eventually, the federal government passed a $2 trillion package to bolster the economy. They sent each person living in the United States a check for two grand.

Some businesses started using Zoom meetings for employees to communicate during the day. Legal documents were being executed using DocuSign. Somehow, people were figuring out how to stay in business, and those who still had jobs were working from home. Every day, more people were dying, and the news was consumed by Covid all day, every day.

With an unimaginable situation like this, our instincts were to go to our children and grandchildren to help and protect them. But we were told that traveling was the worst thing to do and that we should "shelter in place." We were fortunate to be in sunny Florida, where we could at least enjoy outdoor activities. Lori and John invited us out on the boat a few more times.

By May, the governor of Florida allowed restaurants to reopen if they had outdoor seating. Many did. Many others would block off sidewalks to set up tables. We wondered if there was a similar response to the Spanish Flu, which swept the country a hundred years previously.

With everyone staying home with some extra cash, new business opportunities were opening up. People were moving out of cities to the country where they could work from home on their computers, as long as there was internet. Amazon sales were skyrocketing. Grocery and restaurant delivery services were booming. But people were continuing to die at the rate of nearly fifty thousand a month. Twice that number were sick or hospitalized.

It was nearing the end of May and getting hot in southern Florida. We planned to drive back to Westchester because we feared getting on a plane. We decided to hang around for the board meeting at the end of May. We were told there would be one, but everyone must wear masks and stay six feet apart. Many people had already left, so this plan seemed feasible. Jim and Karen left to care for her niece because Karen's sister had contracted Covid and was hospitalized.

The meeting started as usual. By now, we were all accustomed to wearing masks and spacing ourselves out. All the board members were there, spread out among two tables. After the waiver of reading the minutes and the financial report, Dave announced that the engineer had not been out yet due to Covid. He also announced that we would be reopening the pools on a limited basis. They had consulted with the health department along with our attorney. We could use the swimming pool with a limit of ten people in the water at any time. The Jacuzzi limit would be two people. They would only put out half the lounge chairs to maintain the six-foot separation.

He continued by saying that they were looking into setting up a Zoom account so we could hold our meetings remotely. The room remained quiet except for some questions about complying with the new pool rules. With no other business, the meeting was adjourned. Over the next few days, signs went up informing us of our new Covid rules.

Hannah and I enjoyed one more afternoon at the pool, relishing the contrast of warm sun and refreshing water. That evening, we packed up the Mazda and prepared our unit for the summer. The following morning, we headed home. While driving, we made a hotel reservation in North Carolina for an overnight stop right off the highway. Hannah had thoughtfully packed our pillowcases because we feared we'd catch Covid from the ones at a hotel. Once we checked in, we had difficulty finding an open restaurant. The desk clerk gave us a list of places nearby that would deliver, and that evening, we shared a pizza in our room with Diet Cokes. The following day, on our home stretch, the traffic around New York City was nonexistent, which was the one positive thing on our journey home.

SUMMER 2020

Over the summer, Covid seemed to dominate every aspect of American life. According to news reports, it was the same way throughout the world. The work-from-home trend had taken over, and everyone seemed to be getting a dog. More and more people were moving to places like Florida, Colorado, and Vermont. If you were working from home, there was no reason to pay the big rents in the cities when you could live in the places you go to on vacation. Your whole life could be a vacation!

According to the real estate market reports I was still receiving, values in New York City were tanking, while values in Florida and some rural states were rising. I'd seen many boom-and-bust cycles in my years in real estate, but this was a boom in some areas and a bust in others—very unusual.

We were notified that there would be no board meeting in June, but a Zoom meeting was planned for the last Saturday in July.

In early July, Hannah received a phone call from Karen—they'd stayed in touch. Karen called with the news that her sister had died, and she was now the legal guardian of her niece, Jackie. I could see tears in Hannah's eyes, and I assumed Karen was crying on the other end of the line. Karen told Hannah that she hadn't figured out what she would do but would keep in touch. I comforted Hannah the best I could by letting her talk it all out.

We got together with our kids and grandkids almost every week, and I was playing golf in the Sprain Brook league. The new thing in golf was to leave the flagstick in while putting to prevent the spread of germs from touching the stick. Weird.

The end of July rolled around, and Hannah and I sat at the computer to see if the Oceanside Zoom meeting would work. We could see Diane's face when it opened on the screen, but that was about it. A little while later, other faces popped up, but we could only hear a few of them. It took everyone a while to figure out how to unmute themselves, but in time, we were up and running. The board completed the usual waiving of the minutes and the financial statement. Then Dave Davis moved on to old business. First up was the engineer's report concerning our patio decks.

"The engineer tells us that the decks are in bad shape and will never pass next year's recertification. I asked him what he would charge to develop a repair plan and a bid package."

Diane told us the engineer had sent us an estimate of $25,000 for the testing and design, and estimated another $25,000 to do all the required inspections during the repairs. The reactions of dismay were noticeable, even over the computer feed, but nothing like what it would have been like in person. Dave opened a question and comment session.

"Did he tell you how much the work will cost?" demanded one man whose face wasn't on the screen.

Dave replied, "I asked, but once again, he told me he could not give us a number without completing the plan, but other projects he had done like this ran about five million."

Now, we could clearly hear some pushback. "This is on top of the nine and a half million we have already committed to?"

"That is correct," Dave answered.

This time, we heard swearing. We could only imagine how dramatic this would have been in person. I felt bad for the board members—they were dealing with all this for nothing. Not even a reserved parking space.

Discussion on this matter went on for quite a while. Many of the residents thought we now needed to reconsider the bank financing. The fifteen million dollar bill might be too much to handle, even if we did four payments. George said he and Dave would meet with the bank again and report back at the next meeting.

Dave then offered, "I might have some good news. I heard from the attorneys yesterday. They told me that Islandia had upped their offer to two million. Our attorneys are advising us to take it."

Because this meeting was on Zoom, the reaction was not immediately apparent. Each person had to be recognized and speak one at a time. Some people were happy that this was coming at just the right time to help with the assessment, while others expressed dismay. "We are asking for ten million. Two million is letting them off easy," one person said.

After more opinions were expressed, George stated that he thought it was a good offer and that we should take it.

"I propose that we table this for a month," Dave declared. "I'll ask Diane to e-mail a survey out to all owners. While it is the board's responsibility to make the decision, I would like a sense of everyone's thinking." He asked for a motion, which was made, seconded, and passed. Dave continued, "Okay. Next month's meeting will be a big one. I hope most of you will be Zooming in."

And at that, the meeting was adjourned.

As we enjoyed our summer in Westchester, I continued to watch the real estate listings for the Miami area online. I saw sales closing in Oceanside for fifty percent more than the previous year. It appeared that since all the units in the newer buildings were selling for two million and up, it was dragging the prices in our building up along with it—even with the upcoming assessment! I showed some of these listings to Hannah.

"Maybe we should think about selling too," she suggested.

"It's worth thinking about. But we just love it there so much."

Hannah nodded her head. "We do."

When we received the email asking our opinion about the offer from Islandia, I responded in the affirmative that we should accept the offer.

As the end of August rolled around, It was again time for a board meeting. We received the agenda and a link for the Zoom meeting a few days ahead.

On Saturday, I joined the meeting on my own. Hannah was out at yoga, preferring exercise over drama. Launching the Zoom meeting was still a little shaky, but after a few minutes, we all were connected. Once we finished all the preliminaries, Dave and George reported on the meeting with the bank. They told us that the bank was willing to make the fifteen million dollar loan, and the payments would be $201,000 per month for seven years at 3.5 percent interest. "That breaks out to an average payment per unit of about one thousand dollars per month or three thousand per quarter. Of course, it will be less for the one-bedroom units and more for the three-bedroom penthouses."

Dave asked, "What are all your thoughts?"

Each person spoke up one at a time, and it was evident that the majority favored the plan. Then, I saw Jim on the Zoom screen. He asked, "What total interest will we pay over the seven years?"

"One point nine million," George answered. He seemed to have all the numbers in his head or right in front of him.

Someone else said, "That's just about what we will get from Islandia."

Dave said, "That's true, but let's not get ahead of ourselves."

The questions and comments went on for another few minutes. I sensed that bank financing was the way we would go. Dave asked for a motion to table that subject for a month while they worked on the details. The motion carried.

"The next order of business is the Islandia offer," Dave announced. "Our engineer asked me about this. He told me our attorneys contacted him a few weeks ago and asked if he would testify in court for us. He told them that he would, but he would only be able to say that the drilling had undoubtedly contributed to the problems here, but the primary problem was rust and corrosion due to moisture."

There were a few more questions and angry comments.

"Can I have a motion to accept the offer?"

George made the motion. Tom seconded it.

"All in favor?"

Dave and George raised their hands and said, "Aye."

Looking slightly surprised, Dave continued, "All those opposed?"

Lindsay, Tom, and Bob Randazzo raised their hands. "Nay."

"The motion fails," Dave spoke curtly. "I'll notify our attorneys."

George's face turned red. From what I could see on the Zoom screen, almost everyone was shocked. Accepting this offer seemed like a no-brainer to me.

There wasn't any other business, so the meeting adjourned. I called Jim on the phone to ask his opinion of the meeting.

"I'm in total disbelief," he said. "That was complete horse shit."

"Thank you. I agree. Turning down that offer was a big mistake!"

We chatted about it for a little while until we calmed down. I ended the call by saying, "I'm sure Hannah will call Karen later."

When Hannah got home, I told her all about the meeting. She was also surprised about us turning down the Islandia offer. She said she'd call Karen later.

That afternoon, after she had spoken with Karen, she told me that they were thinking about returning to Florida soon to get Jackie enrolled in school. She would be starting her sophomore year in high school.

A week went by, and we got an official e-mail from Diane. It was a call for candidates. It appeared George had resigned.

FALL 2020

O nce the leaves started to turn, we were reminded that it was about time to head back to Florida. This year, we would be driving. Even if we were willing to take a plane, all our cars were in Westchester. We decided to make it a leisurely trip and spend a few days on the road, stopping at places that intrigued us. On the last Saturday of September, we skipped the board meeting altogether.

We were still fearful of Covid in early October but packed up our belongings anyhow, and hit the road. Our first stop was Baltimore, where we settled at a hotel in the inner harbor for the night. Eager to indulge in a local delicacy, we went out for steamed blue crabs. Our waitress showed us how to eat them. They were spicy, a bit of work, and a total mess! But we loved them. Noticing the tables around us, it appeared customary to order a bucket of Corona beer bottles along with the crabs—a perfect combination.

As we continued south the following day, we veered off I-95 and meandered along the coastal route with no real destination in mind. Eventually, we found ourselves in New Bern, North Carolina—a delightful coastal town with more churches and parks than usual for a town this size. We discovered it was also the birthplace of Pepsi. We found a hotel overlooking the docks and enjoyed dinner at an Irish pub.

We got up early the following day, hoping to make it to Savannah, Georgia. Our GPS route had guided us to a ferry crossing a river and through lowlands. The small, open ferry was a unique experience, complete with the chain placed across the ramps once we got underway. We sat in the car the whole way, admiring the scenery and appreciating the novelty of our shared experience.

By mid-afternoon, we made it to Savannah. We checked into a hotel and took a trolley tour of the city. Our guide regaled us with stories of the city's historic buildings and intriguing folk-lore. On the tour, we heard about a candle-lit basement pub. Of course, that was where we had dinner, and it took a while for our eyes to adjust to the darkness. Once we could see enough so we wouldn't trip and fall, the hostess sat us in a wine cellar, where there was a very romantic table for two.

We had a leisurely drive the next day to St. Augustine. Once again, we hopped on a trolley tour around the city, stop-ping at the "Fountain of Youth." Our hotel was conveniently located in the town center, allowing us to explore some areas we saw on our trolley tour. Finally, we had dinner at a restaurant that looked interesting from the tour.

With a six-hour drive ahead of us the following day, we aimed to reach Miami—our last leg of the road trip. We arrived at our condo by mid-afternoon, and Hannah immediately made the beds, cleaned the bathrooms, and dusted the tables. I couldn't imagine where she had found the energy to clean—I was exhausted from five days on the road. I felt guilty sitting around, so I went to the grocery store. For the remainder of the day, all we did was lounge around. After dinner, we went for a walk on the beach, happy to be back. We noticed along the way the signs limiting the use of the pool were still in place.

Hannah and I stopped by the office in the morning to say hello to Diane. We chatted through our masks about the meeting we missed. She told us the board unanimously approved the bank financing plan, and they had voted to start charging the payments next month to build up some funds before the work began. "You'll be getting a notice with your payment amount soon." She also explained that the engineer had completed the plans and bid package for the patio decks. I asked about George and the board member opening.

"Are you thinking about running?" she asked, a bit of hope in her eyes.

I guess I foolishly left myself wide open for that. "No, I'm just curious as to why he resigned."

"He says he is just fed up with the people around here and could not understand how they could not jump at the two-million-dollar settlement offer from Islandia."

"Well, I can agree with him there," I said. "I thought we should have taken it as well."

"Are you both retired?" Diane asked.

"Yes, we are," I answered.

"What did you do for a career?" she prodded.

I told her I was in real estate and Hannah was a teacher.

"Real estate, huh? You'd be perfect for the board. And Hannah, you have experience keeping a classroom in order. You'd be good as well."

We both looked at each other, realizing what we had stepped into. "I don't think we would be interested," I said. "We'd be concerned about personal liability if something were to go wrong around here."

She informed us they have an insurance policy to protect directors and officers. Additionally, the association would indemnify us for anything the insurance doesn't cover. "It's all in the condo's legal documents," she concluded.

"We'll think about it and let you know," I said as we walked away, feeling like we were being strong-armed.

We spent the rest of the morning at the pool, sitting side by side in our lounge chairs, six feet away from the other residents in the area. It was my night to cook, so I told Hannah, "I'm planning to make spaghetti carbonara for dinner. I'm sure I can make enough if you'd like to invite Jim and Karen."

She reminded me that her niece was staying with them. I thought a moment, figured we'd have enough for five, and said, "No problem; I'd like to meet her."

She took out her phone and made the call. After the call ended, she said, "They'll all be up around six. Karen is bringing a salad."

Later that afternoon, I started prepping for the carbonara while sipping a vodka tonic. It would all be last-minute cooking, so it helped to prepare everything beforehand. I pre-cooked the bacon, chopped a shallot, grated some parmesan, and thawed the peas. I also took out four eggs so they would be at room temperature when I was ready to cook.

When our guests arrived, Karen exclaimed, "It smells good in here." They introduced Jackie, and we sat on the patio with vodka tonics while Jackie had a Sprite. Hannah asked her how she liked her new school. Jackie told us she was enjoying it and that she'd made the varsity cheerleading team.

"Wow, as a sophomore?" Hannah praised. "You must be pretty good."

"I tried out just hoping to make new friends, but I made the team!" She told us she had been on the gymnastics team last year and was pretty nimble. She was not shy at all—in fact, just the opposite. She informed us that she was fifteen and a half, and her birthday was in January. We all enjoyed her company and let her lead the conversation.

I thought to myself, She seems to show no ill effects from the trauma of losing her mother. I was certainly not going to bring it up, but I hoped she was dealing with it in a mentally healthy way.

I excused myself to cook, and Karen joined me in the kitchen to plate the salad. We all sat down at the dining room table when dinner was ready. Jim poured some chardonnay they had brought, and we all dug in.

"This is fantastic," Karen remarked.

"Thank you. So is the salad," I replied.

As we ate, Hannah brought up the conversation we had with Diane.

"Are you going to do it?" Karen questioned.

"I'm not," Hannah announced. "I'm not sure about Bob," she added, looking at me with raised eyebrows.

Jim and Karen both looked at me with a similar questioning expression.

"I never really considered it," I said. "It always seems like a zoo down there."

Jim remarked, "It doesn't sound like you've ruled it out."

"We'll see," I said, hoping for a change of subject.

After dinner and decaf coffee, we all said goodnight and told Jackie how wonderful it was to meet her.

I added, "Good luck with the cheerleading."

The following day, I received a call from Dave Davis, the board president. He told me that Diane recommended he call me regarding the board seat.

"Yes, we did discuss it, but I hadn't given it much thought."

He asked if I would meet him in the social room to talk about it.

"Okay, when were you thinking?"

"Any time. Now is fine with me."

I replied hesitantly, "Give me half an hour, and I'll meet you there."

Hannah had overheard the phone call. She looked at me, waiting for me to speak.

"It's just a conversation," I claimed.

"Uh-huh," she said, clearly unconvinced.

I changed my shirt and went downstairs to meet Dave. His sales pitch was pretty good. He praised me for my work on the contractor selection committee and thought my real estate background would be helpful. He confirmed what Diane had told me about the liability insurance and told me I wouldn't have to be elected—they could just appoint me.

I just sat there, taking it all in, then said, "Let me talk this out with Hannah, and I'll let you know tomorrow."

We rose and shook hands.

"I look forward to hearing from you," he said as we departed.

I went back upstairs to find Hannah waiting for me.

"So you are considering it?" she asked.

"Maybe," I replied.

"Uh-huh," she teased again.

We went down to the beach for the rest of the day, bringing an umbrella, a cooler, and our chairs. We discussed the pros and cons of my joining the board, and I felt an element of responsibility to consider it. She helped me talk through my decision like she always does.

When I woke up in the morning, I realized I had decided to be on the board, to do my part. After breakfast, I called Dave and told him the news. He thanked me profusely and said he would introduce me at the next board meeting. He went on to ask if I had any time in the next few days to meet with him so he could bring me up to date on the inner workings of the board and his vision of what our focus should be. I agreed to meet in his unit the following morning.

Later that day, we saw Diane, who smiled at us knowingly. Then, Hannah called Karen and updated her about my decision. Hannah told me that Karen thought I'd be good on the board.

So there you have it. I was going to be part of the Oceanside shit show!

I knocked on Dave's door the following day at nine. He welcomed me in and re-introduced his wife, Kathleen. We had previously met, and I had seen her around the building but had never spoken with her at any length. She served us coffee in the living room and then disappeared.

After a few moments of pleasantries, Dave got down to business. "Now that you are officially on the board, I wanted to impress upon you the depth of our structural issues."

That statement got my attention, and I listened intently as he continued.

"George and I are the only ones who have walked the property with the engineer, as he showed us the severity of the concrete deterioration. As you might know, no more than two board members can meet without an official meeting being posted for the entire membership to be invited. I have tried my best to convey my concerns to each board member individually, as I am doing with you today, but I don't think I have gotten through to them. I desperately fear that the pool deck could collapse into the garage."

By now, I was riveted.

He went on. "Too many of the residents and some of the board members feel it is their duty to keep our assessments as low as possible, and I get that, but this is now dangerous. That's why George resigned from the board: we weren't getting through to these people. It was the last straw for him when we turned down the two million dollar settlement."

"What can I do to help?" I offered.

"We need to somehow get the work started ASAP. In these meetings, we quibble about how to best pay for it, resulting in more delays."

I asked, "When is the next time the engineer is coming out? I'd like to meet him."

We have nothing scheduled, but I'd like you to join us the next time he does. I'll let you know."

"Good. As you know, I've been around real estate my whole life, so maybe I'll understand some of it better than others."

"That's what I hoped. Another problem is this nit-wit Bob Randazzo and his building inspector friend. Our engineer tells me this inspector knows nothing and can't understand how he got his job."

"Well, that's encouraging," I said sarcastically.

"Randazzo is not someone we need on the board right now. He is going to fight spending money until the building falls down!"

"I understand. We'll just need to keep everyone else on the board informed to offset his vote. You can count on my support, Dave."

"Thanks, Bob. Go down and look at the columns and beams yourself some time. You'll easily see the rust and decay."

"I'll do that. This meeting has been a real eye-opener."

I got up to leave, and he thanked me for hearing him out.

"I'll be in touch soon," I said, walking out the door.

As I returned to my unit, I wondered what I had gotten myself into. I saw Hannah as soon as I entered.

"What happened? You look like you've seen a ghost," she quizzed.

"You can't believe what Dave just shared with me. He is really concerned about the delays in the concrete repairs. He's afraid the pool deck might collapse."

"What did we get ourselves into here, Bob?"

"That's exactly what I'm asking myself," I replied, shaking my head.

Later that day, I went down to the garage and inspected the columns and beams. I noticed chunks of concrete missing, and more was loose and flaking. Beneath that, I could see exposed steel rebar that was severely rusting. It was apparent to me that it needed repair, but I would have needed to be an engineer to measure the remaining strength of the members, and I was not.

At the October meeting, I was introduced to everyone in attendance. The Zoom thing was still happening, but the whole board and many residents were there in person, still trying to stay six feet apart. After the preliminaries, we got down to old business. First up was the Islandia suit. Dave informed us that our lawyers told him we would now play the waiting game. They would start preparing to go to court if we didn't hear anything soon. The next order of business was selecting a contractor for the patio deck repairs.

He addressed Diane. "How should we go about this?"

Diane said that she had spoken to our attorney and that we could modify our existing contract with Blue Water and avoid the three-bid requirement.

"Thank you, Diane. Can I have a motion to modify our existing contract with Blue Water?"

Tom made the motion, and I said, "I'll second it."

Hannah smiled at me—my first official act as a board member.

"All in favor?" asked Dave.

We all raised our hands and declared, "Aye."

The vote was unanimous.

I then asked Dave if I could speak. "Sure, the floor is yours," he replied.

"When we speak to the contractor, can we ask if it makes sense to temporarily shore up the beam in the garage until the work begins?"

Before Dave could reply, Bob Randazzo declared, "That will just add more to the bill, and we already heard from Mr. Tomasi that it's unnecessary."

Dave spoke up, "I'm not sure that's exactly what he said, Bob. I will ask the engineer for his thoughts when I see him."

The rest of the meeting was uneventful. There was discussion about relaxing the Covid rules, but no changes were made. We had all become accustomed to them by now. Before adjourning, Dave announced that the board would go into an "executive session" to elect a new treasurer. We adjourned and shut down the Zoom feed while those in attendance filed out.

With just the board in the room, Dave asked, "Would anyone like to be treasurer?"

Tom spoke up and offered, "I'm not an accountant like George, but I had plenty of accounting classes at business school. I think I could handle it."

"Thank you, Tom. Anyone else?"

Crickets.

"Okay, Tom will be our new treasurer. I am happy to remain as president if no one objects?"

No one objected.

"Lindsay can remain secretary and Bob Randazzo a director, if that is okay?" No one objected. He looked at me and asked, "Bob Osborne, will you be vice president?"

I agreed. Wait until I tell Hannah, I thought.

We adjourned, and Lindsay provided Diane with all the necessary details for the minutes. Although my involvement so far was minimal, the association seemed to be moving forward despite the pending lawsuit. We had hired a contractor to do the long overdue work and had a plan to pay for it. Having looked at the decaying concrete myself, however, we would just need to focus on getting the job started soon.

November had arrived, and I continued to monitor the real estate listings online. To my surprise, some three-bedroom units at Oceanside were selling for well over a million dollars, and a two-bedroom like ours had closed for $750,000. I couldn't help but be amazed at the prices these units were fetching, considering everyone was aware of the assessments.

The first of November rolled around, and it was time to plan for the holidays. We were pleased to be invited for Thanksgiving at Lori and John's again. This year, they invited Jim, Karen, and Jackie as well. We had a lovely time, and it sounded like Jackie was enjoying school down here.

We flew home for Christmas. This was our first time on a plane since Covid. We wore masks and sanitized our hands and everything else we might touch on the plane. We were happy that they were still not filling the middle seats. As usual, we had a wonderful time with our family. The grandkids had grown so much this year. They were attending class on their computers from home, but it was clear that they missed the social interactions with their classmates.

WINTER/SPRING 2021

The first week of January, we flew back to Miami—just in time for the crowds. It was announced that vaccines were now available and that we "senior citizens" would be the first to get them for free. We were hopeful that the vaccine would return all our lives back to normal. The county had a website you could use to make an appointment. Of course, it crashed immediately. We were told to go on the website at six a.m. and pick a time. This was easier said than done. The site was overloaded, and all the appointments were gone by the time it was our turn in the queue. We heard of some people having luck, but we sure didn't, and we became increasingly frustrated. Getting an appointment for a vaccine was like finding paper towels at Publix. Hannah finally got an appointment the last week in January. I got one the first week in February but would have to drive to Hollywood. We felt like we had finally conquered the system!

Our board meeting at the end of January went smoothly. The social room was about half full, and most everyone else was on Zoom. We talked about the schedule for the construction work, and we assured everyone that it would not start until after Easter. Many residents rented their units out for high season and didn't want the work to disturb their tenants. They were charging over four thousand dollars per month with a three-month minimum. I could understand that the renters might not have much tolerance for the noise and the mess—it would definitely disturb the peace. We told everyone that the construction would take at least a year.

We also outlined each resident's responsibility regarding removing their patio furniture and hurricane shutters. Diane explained that she would send instructions and an estimate of when it would be done. Some people were still complaining about paying the assessments, but that was a done deal. If they had to sell, they would enjoy a handsome profit. Dave answered specific questions about the engineer's plan the best he could. Overall, this was the most peaceful meeting I had witnessed. When the meeting adjourned, everyone filed out in a good mood.

We heard about one of the penthouse units selling for 1.5 million dollars, even with a three-thousand-dollar monthly assessment fee on top of the HOA dues!

I really started watching the listings now. This felt like a bubble to me.

Over cocktails one evening, I mentioned to Hannah my thoughts on the current real estate market. In all my years of professional experience, there were only a few times when it experienced huge price increases. The first occurrence that came to mind was in the late eighties, followed by another in the mid-2000s. On both occasions, the market went down substantially shortly thereafter. It appeared that we were amid one of those booming periods to me. We were witnessing a perfect storm of changing demand, excess available money, and the lowest interest rates I'd ever seen.

"It sounds like you think we should sell," Hannah stated.

"Maybe we should think about it," I replied.

"Okay, we will. But let's not rush it."

"No rush."

Over the next few weeks, I tried to remain calm when we spoke about selling our condo. I kept showing her the listings in our building—what they were asking and getting. If we sold our unit, we would nearly double our money in four years. I knew from experience that only occurs a few times in a lifetime. I also knew February was close to peak selling season—especially in Florida, with the snowbirds down here.

I brought the subject up again over cocktails one afternoon on our patio overlooking the ocean.

"But where would we go?" Hannah asked.

"We could winter in Spain," I suggested. "Or how about Portugal on the Algarve?"

"Oh, Bob, you're such a dreamer."

"Or how about we put the money in the bank and go on a month-long cruise? We could also just leave the money in the bank for a few years, come back here, and buy another place. At least we won't be around for all the construction," I added.

"You're getting serious, aren't you?"

"I guess I am."

We continued going to the pool or the beach each day. As time passed, the restaurants figured out how to deal with Covid better. Now that we had the vaccine, we felt more comfortable going out. We had dinner with Jim and Karen or Lori and John just about every week. I would forward Hannah the real estate listings or some articles about Portugal to her email. She could tell I was getting serious and was beginning to open her mind to the idea.

While she was opening her mind, I was getting a fever!

Another evening on the patio, she brought up the subject.

"Are you sure that if we sell, we'll be able to afford something like this again?"

I considered her question for a moment. "I can't guarantee it, but I'll bet we'll find something even better."

"If we put it on the market, how much should we ask?"

"I'm not sure," I replied. "Maybe I should call Marie."

"Do that. Invite her to lunch. Let's see what she thinks."

I picked my phone up off the table and made the call.

"Bob, how are you?" she answered.

"Just fine, Marie. It's good to hear your voice."

"How are you and Hannah enjoying the winter?" she inquired.

"Great," I replied. "I'm calling to invite you to lunch to discuss listing our unit."

"Sure, I'd love to see you two. How about the day after tomorrow?"

"That would be fine," I confirmed. "Does twelve-thirty work?"

"See you then."

I told Hannah that Marie was coming the day after tomorrow.

"I'll have to go out tomorrow to get salad makings," she said.

The following afternoon, we went to the pool to meet Jim and Karen. I knew Hannah had been sharing our plans with

Karen. The two of them were becoming as thick as thieves. Both Jim and Karen were curious about our line of thought. They knew I had spent my career in real estate and were trying to pick my brain. I shared the recent selling prices of the units here. They were as surprised as I was that they were selling for those prices, even with the vast assessment and upcoming construction. After a while in the sun, Jim and I went swimming in the ocean, leaving the ladies to chat by themselves. When we returned, they were in the pool with some of their friends from Yoga.

By late afternoon, Karen told us she needed to pick up Jackie at school, and Jim left with her. When the sun started to set, Hannah and I went up for a shower and some cocktails. After getting out of the shower, Hannah asked me to put some lotion on her back. As I was doing that, I started becoming aroused. That's happened before. *Oh, well. The cocktails can wait.*

The following day, Marie rang the bell right at 12:30. As I recall, she was always punctual. She came in, and we fist bumped, the new greeting post-Covid.

As Marie handed Hannah a bottle of chilled rosé, she remarked, "I love what you've done with the place."

Hannah led Marie into the living room while I opened the wine.

"This building is becoming quite popular," Marie exclaimed.

"Yes, we are seeing that," Hannah agreed, "and becoming quite valuable too."

"That it is," Marie affirmed. "So, are you guys are thinking about selling?"

I answered, "It depends. What do you think the condo is worth?"

"Well, I took a look at the comps this morning. Completely redone like this, I would think, somewhere in the eight-hundreds."

"You are aware of the assessment?" I asked.

"Yes. Most buildings this age have assessments. With the newer buildings selling for two million and up, it is still quite affordable."

We brought our wine glasses to the table, and Hannah served an arugula and artichoke heart salad with red and gold beets drizzled with Dijon vinaigrette.

"This is lovely," Marie told Hannah.

"Thanks, enjoy."

I asked Marie, "If we were to sell in the price range you indicated, what should we ask?"

"Well, the real estate marketing model has changed in the last year or so. Nowadays, you list it low and look for a bidding war."

"Really? We always used to ask a little more, so you had room to negotiate."

"That's right," Marie agreed. "I spent my whole life doing business like that. The industry has changed." She picked up a folder and showed me a few listings. "See this one? It was listed at a million five and closed for a million seven."

I put on the readers that were conveniently hanging around my neck and looked at the listing.

"Here is another one. It listed at six ninety-nine and sold for seven hundred and fifty thousand."

"So, if we were to put this one on the market, what do you recommend?" I asked.

"Seven ninety-nine. You will get offers over the asking price immediately. I think it will bid up close to eight hundred fifty thousand before we're done."

I looked at Hannah and asked her if she wanted to sleep on it.

She replied, "Let's list it. That's a lot of money."

Marie, being the professional I knew she was, had brought a listing form with her. She filled it out, and we all signed right there.

"Can I refill your wine, ladies?" I asked.

"Cheers," they both exclaimed as we touched our glasses.

We chatted for a few more minutes, and Marie said, "I've got to run. I want to get this in the system today."

Hannah had to share the news with both Karen and Lori. When she finished her calls, we sat outside watching the ocean.

"I'm going to miss this," she said with regret.

"Me too. But there are plenty of beaches in the world."

Hannah laughed. "You're a real philosopher, Bob."

I just smiled. A few minutes later, we walked down to the Asian fusion place for a California roll and an order of spicy chicken.

The following morning, we cleaned our unit and put things away so it would be ready for showings. We decided to head down to the beach but stopped by the office to tell Diane we had listed our unit. I wanted to be the one to tell her before she heard it elsewhere.

"Really? You've only been on the board for two meetings."

"I know. How do we handle that?"

She told me I could stay on the board until the closing. "I'll let Dave know so he can look for another candidate. I'm sure it will sell right away in this market."

Over the next week, we had half a dozen showings. On the second day, we had our first offer of $810, which was pretty good for an opener. The following offer was $825, better yet. We got another for $840, and our joy continued to grow. At the end of the week, Marie called. She told me she would like to ask each party to give us their highest and best offers by noon tomorrow.

"When would you like to close?" she asked.

Usually, we would be looking for as soon as possible, but in this case, we thought we'd like to stay through the season. I asked Hannah.

"How about through Easter?"

I relayed that to Marie.

"Easter is on the fourth of April this year. Shall we say the sixth?"

I told her that was fine with us.

"Okay, I'll make that clear to the interested parties. I'll let you know how we make out tomorrow afternoon."

We said our goodbyes and hung up. *I love a seller's market!*

The following afternoon, Marie called. "I have an all-cash offer for you of $851,000 with no contingencies. Closing date to be on the sixth of April."

"Bingo. You were right on the money, Marie!"

"I thought you'd be happy. Can I stop by later for your signatures?"

"Sure, what time is good for you?" I asked.

"How about three-thirty?"

"Perfect, see you then."

I told Hannah the good news. She seemed happy, but I could tell her mind had already leaped to what would have to be done before moving out. Marie arrived promptly at three-thirty. We signed the contract, and I asked her if she had time for a drink.

"Thanks, but I want to get this to the title office before they close." And off she went.

Hannah and I went out on the patio and started making a list of things to do. I knew she could obsess over tasks like this, so I just helped her think things through and offered to help with anything I could. I knew she would be content by tomorrow.

When I went down to get the mail the following morning, I saw Dave standing at the office door, speaking with Diane. I stood alongside him and waited for a pause in their conversation.

"Good morning," I said, telling them we had a buyer and a closing date.

Dave asked about the selling price.

When I told him, he said, "Excellent, good to hear."

Diane added, "The prices keep going up and up."

"It's good for everyone in the building. At least we know after paying the assessment money that the value will be there," I said, and they both agreed.

Dave asked Diane to send out another "call for candidates" and asked if I would remain on the board for the next two meetings.

"Sure, I'll assist in any way you'd like. By the way, did you ever speak to the engineer about shoring up the garage beam?"

"Yes, we met when you were home at Christmas. I invited Bob Randazzo to join us, hoping he could comprehend the urgency of the repairs. We walked down to the garage to examine the deteriorating beams and columns. As the engineer pointed out the areas of concern, Bob seemed uninterested in what he had to say. It was like he had closed his mind to all of it." He continued, "I did ask the engineer about the shoring, and he said that would be the first thing the contractors do before starting work." Dave thanked me for my service to the association as we wandered out.

We all filed into the social room for the February meeting the following Saturday. Diane handed out the agenda, and the meeting was called to order. After the standard housekeeping, we went on to the old business. The first item on the agenda was the patio deck repairs. Dave stated that we received the final quote from Blue Water, which came in at $4.9 million. "The good news is that we are slightly under our budget of fifteen million that we have the financing for."

The members in the room nodded their heads at the news.

Dave continued, "That will give us some room for any overruns that might come up. And we don't have to use every last cent if we don't need to." Then, he asked, "Are there any comments or questions on this matter before we move on?"

One person in the room raised their hand.

"Yes, Charlie?"

Charlie Mason stood and asked, "If we have any money left over, can we consider updating the façade? Our building looks quite dated compared to the new buildings on the street."

Dave noticed that there seemed to be some agreement in the room. "Can I have a show of hands from those who agree with Charlie?"

Most everyone in the room raised their hands.

"Okay. Obviously, we need to wait until we see if any funds are available once we get into this project. Perhaps we need to form a façade committee."

"I am willing to be on that committee," offered Charlie.

A few of the ladies raised their hands as well. Dave asked us for a motion to table this until the next meeting. I made the motion, and Lindsay seconded it. It carried unanimously.

Dave asked Charlie, "Can you put a few people together and share your thoughts at the next meeting?"

"I'll be happy to, Dave," Charlie answered.

"Great. Please remember that it could be a year or more before we know if we will have any funds."

The next item on the agenda was the Islandia lawsuit. Dave said, "We have nothing to report at this time."

There was no response in the room. *That item will stay on every agenda until it is resolved,* I thought.

"Okay," Dave said. "Since we don't have any new business, we can open the floor for member discussion."

There were some questions about pool rules and rules about service dogs—the usual stuff that Diane could usually handle by speaking to the people directly after the meeting. When it quieted down, Dave asked for a motion to adjourn. A minute later, we were filing out of the room.

At the beginning of March, Hannah and I were focused on getting rid of our furniture and household items. The appliances, of course, would stay with the unit. Marie had informed us that her buyers wanted our entire guest bedroom set. They offered us $750 for it, and we accepted. We put a notice on the bulletin board by the mailboxes that we wanted to sell everything else. The response was more than we expected, but everything we had was only four years old and still in style, so we had buyers for almost everything. Even the pots and pans!

We would keep only the personal items we could pack in the car. Everything else would go to the Humane Society Charity Store. Regarding the furnishings we were still using, it was agreed that whoever was buying it could pick it up the day after Easter. Having all that resolved took a big load off Hannah's shoulders, and she was back to her usual fun-loving self.

We went to the beach almost every day to get our fill. We hung out with Jim and Karen most days and visited Lori and John a few times. We each got our second Covid vaccine the second week in March. The month flew by, and once again, it was time for the board meeting.

Hannah came along this time and sat with Karen and Jim. Dave started the meeting, Tom read through the financial statement, and the reading of last month's minutes was waived. As usual, old business was first on the agenda. There was still nothing to report on the Islandia lawsuit.

The next item was the construction work. Dave informed us that Blue Water intended to start work in mid-May after the snowbirds and renters were gone. He told us that we had paid them $750,000 as a deposit. We were now committed, and they could start moving equipment on-site next month. Next up was the façade committee. Dave asked Charlie to lead this discussion.

He and another owner, Claire, expressed their ideas on what could be done at a reasonable cost. A few other people tossed out a few different Ideas.

Dave asked if anyone else would like to be on the committee. Karen raised her hand along with Tom's wife, Kate. Dave suggested that a board member should also be on the committee. Tom volunteered, so that was our façade committee. Dave led us through the formal motions and the vote. It passed unanimously. He reminded everyone that it would be a while until there would be a budget.

Dave announced that this would be my last meeting and expressed appreciation for my contributions. I received a round of applause and comments that I would be missed, but I was sure I would be forgotten pretty quickly. I stood and thanked everyone for their friendship and kind words. Before sitting, I added, "Before I leave, as my last action on this board, I implore you to have the contractors shore up the beams in the garage as soon as possible. It shouldn't cost any additional money because, as the engineer explained, they have to do it anyway."

There were a few nods of agreement, and then Dave asked for new candidates to take my place. No one jumped out of their seats. The meeting wound down, went through the adjournment process, and we all filed out. A few people stopped Hannah and me, giving us their best wishes and telling us how much they enjoyed having us here. There were some people we would surely miss, but most of all, we would have fond memories of the warm weather and the ocean.

Lori and John invited us up to their place for Easter. Olivia would be joining us, too. We had a week remaining in Florida, so we spent our mornings packing and the afternoons at the beach or the pool, enjoying our last week at Oceanside. When we realized we didn't need all the finishings we thought we did, we called some people who wanted the stuff and let them come early to pick it up. We had the Humane Society scheduled for a pick up on the afternoon of the fifth and our cleaning lady for the morning of the sixth. We were scheduled pretty tight, which made Hannah a bit nervous, but for the next few days, all we had to do was try to relax and enjoy ourselves.

We had a wonderful Easter at Lori and John's. Olivia told us all about her new job in New York and her little apartment in Manhattan. We made plans to have her up to the house in Westchester and invited Lori and John up to visit this summer as well. We didn't stay too late because we knew we had a busy day ahead.

On Monday, things actually went as planned. Everyone came to pick up their stuff, and the Humane Society Truck showed up at three o'clock. We now had no place to sit and no

TV to watch. Thankfully, we still had the guest room bed to sleep in for the night. Jim and Karen invited us for dinner, and we sat out on their patio with cocktails, enjoying our last evening with them, gazing at the ocean. Jackie told us all about school and her cheerleading team—they hoped to make the state tournament at the end of the school year. I wasn't even aware there was a cheerleading competition, but you learn something new every day. After a wonderful meal, we discussed how much we would all miss each other. Hannah and I invited them to visit this summer, and they invited us to visit next winter. We had made some good friends during our time there.

When we returned to our unit, we couldn't help but go to bed early. After all, we had nothing to sit on out on the patio. The following morning, we finished packing the car, let our cleaning lady in, and gave the keys to Diane in the office. We weren't required to attend the closing, so we hopped in the car and headed north.

We hoped to make it to Savannah and have dinner at that candle-lit pub again. The traffic was light, and we made it there easily.

On the drive home, we talked about our plans for next winter. We had an open invitation to stay with Lori and John, and we could visit Jim and Karen. I also mentioned renting a VRBO in Costa Rica for a month. We had heard it was nice, and many Americans were moving there.

Once we got home, it took us no time at all to get back into our routine in Westchester. Hannah spoke to Karen on the phone every week, who told her about their plans to head back to Michigan at the end of May when Jackie would be done with school, but now her cheerleading tournament might mean they would stay longer, depending on how far they made it. She also told us the concrete work was delayed a month because some of Blue Water's crews were out with Covid. A few weeks later, when Karen called, she announced that Jackie's team had won the Regionals and would be going on to the State competition. If they won, they would go to the Nationals in June.

We had certainly enjoyed our experience at Oceanside and southern Florida in general. We expected to be back there one way or another soon, and with the friends we made and family there, we felt like we had spread some roots.

I was hopeful that all the work at Oceanside would go as planned.

FIRST RESPONDERS

SUMMER 2021

I could see that the chief had his hands full with every high-ranking public servant in the city surrounding him. I told him I was heading back to check on the progress with the girl and climbed back up the pile. When I arrived, I saw she was awake and in pain. The paramedics assured me that she was stable. Mikey and Carlos had progressed in positioning two lifting bags under the slab. It appeared they had it raised a few inches on one side, but we needed to lift it further. Mikey asked me to place the last bag on the lower side and see if we could lift it higher. After locating a stable area, I filled the bag with air, and it started moving.

"That's it. Easy now. Just a little more. I can look underneath to see what we have. Okay, let's hold it right there," Mikey said. He laid down on his belly and used his flashlight to look underneath. "Okay, it seems like most of the weight is off. I can see a tangle of rebar that appears to be pressing into her leg, but I'm afraid to reach my arm under there. Can someone get me a crowbar so I can try to pry it away?"

I called on my radio with a request for a crowbar. Less than a minute later, Jim climbed up with the bar. Mikey worked the bar under the slab and hooked the rebar. He took a chunk of concrete to use as a fulcrum and pried the rebar out of the way. We heard a moan from the girl. She told us she could feel her leg again, but it hurt even more now. While Mikey held pressure on the bar, I took the flashlight and looked underneath. It seemed like there was free space around her leg. I asked her if she could pull it free.

"It hurts too much. I'm afraid to try."

Carlos asked, "What if we try to pull you out?"

She started to cry but said bravely, "Okay. Let's try it."

Carlos and one of the EMTs each grabbed her under a shoulder and started to ease her out. Mikey kept up the pressure on the crowbar, and I kept watching underneath with the flashlight. They slid her a few inches, and I watched for any change beneath the slab.

"Okay, easy now. Keep it going, real slow," I instructed.

When we had successfully pulled the girl out, I moved in closer to speak with her. She thanked us over and over again and told us her name was Jackie.

The EMTs lifted her onto a stretcher, loaded her into an ambulance, and left for the hospital. I thought to myself, *There goes one. How many more can we save?*

"Nice job," I said to Mikey and Carlos. "Let's get this equipment back on the truck so we know where to find it again."

"You got it, L.T."

There was always a feeling of joy when a life was saved. I took a moment for myself to let it sink in, a rare moment of reward. Then, I looked around at all the activity and began climbing to check in with the other firefighters, eager to learn if they had found any other signs of life. Both Jim and Donnie claimed they had heard some moaning but could not seem to pinpoint its exact location. With at least sixty firefighters now scouring through the rubble, it was clear that we needed to devise an organized plan. When someone lifted or removed a piece of concrete or steel, it was crucial to start a new pile; otherwise, we'd just make things worse. I called the chief on the radio and asked him if he had any ideas. He suggested we start a pile on the west side along the road. That way, when the excavators arrived, they could load it on dump trucks. *Sounds like a plan!* I thought, growing a bit more optimistic about our strategy.

We all returned to picking up pieces manually and carrying them to the new pile, listening for life the whole time. I thought we needed to work for a few minutes, then stop to listen for a few minutes. Maybe we could use microphones or cameras to drop down into the holes.

The first signs of daylight started to show out over the ocean. *Where are the machines?* I wondered.

At 6:30, I heard a tractor-trailer rumbling down the road. I looked around the corner and saw our first excavator arriving. *Hallelujah!* While they were unloading, we kept up the ritual of manually moving pieces of rubble while still listening for signs of survivors. Jim and Donnie thought they heard someone yelling for help, and it seemed they could tell where it was coming from. I and a few other guys went over to work with them in that area. I thought that would be the first spot to send the excavator once he was up and running.

The chief then approached us to see what we had found. Donnie told him what they had heard but that it had been about ten minutes since he'd heard anything. The chief told us to all stop and listen. We did, and within a minute, we all heard the calls for help again. It sounded like it was directly below us. We returned to work, picking through the debris now toward where we thought we heard the sound. We heard the excavator fire up and the *clack-clack-clack* of the tracks heading our way. We saw Chief Williams walk over to the excavator. When the machine stopped, he hopped on the track to speak to the operator. He had taken his respirator off. They seemed to have a somewhat heated discussion, and I could see the Chief was upset. He hopped down and directed the machine toward us.

I asked Mikey to take charge and guide the excavator when lifting the heavy pieces. They could not use the bucket to dig into the rubble, with potential survivors buried in the pile. Mikey seemed to understand the delicacy of the process. He would manually attach chains to the pieces and have the excavator lift them up and out of the way, one at a time. While preparing the chains, the rest of the guys could fill the bucket by hand and have the operator cast them into the pile. It seemed entirely too slow of a process from my perspective.

I could see the chief talking on his cell phone. I walked over to him to learn more about what was happening. He told me this was the only excavator we were going to get. Public Works told him that all their other machines were tied up on a water main break and would not be available until the first of next week. "Ridiculous," he fumed. "Don't they understand there are lives at stake here? This is a once-in-a-lifetime tragedy for this city!"

Since I was out of the worst of the dust, I took my respirator off. All I could do at that moment was look down at my feet as I considered the situation.

"What if we hired an independent contractor?" I asked. "Would the mayor pay for that?"

Chief Williams looked at me for a moment and smiled. "When the press arrives in the next hour, I bet he'll be willing to pay for anything!"

"I know the best excavating machine operators in Southern Florida. The Hauser Brothers," I suggested. "I don't know where they're working, but I'm sure they'll feel it's their civic duty to move some equipment down here and help save some lives."

"Call them. You can tell them I'll guarantee they get paid time and a half!"

I walked back to the engine and dug out my cell phone. It was now 7:00 a.m., and the sun was up. I scrolled through my contacts and called Alex Hauser, whom I'd known since high school. Luckily, he answered on the second ring. He was just climbing into his truck, preparing to start his day. I told him what we were facing and that we needed his help.

"The chief said he would pay you time and a half," I told him.

Alex replied, "Let me see if I can catch Ernie and see where he is. I'll call you right back."

"Thanks, buddy. I'll be standing by."

The press now started to show up in full force. I had noticed a few local reporters on the scene for the last hour, but now the camera crews and networks were setting up. It was about to become a zoo. As I walked back to where I could see the chief talking with his deputy, my phone started to ring. It was Alex.

"Ernie just loaded the Akerman onto the trailer to head up to Davie. He's going to head your way instead. With rush-hour traffic, I guess it'll be at least an hour before he arrives. He'll need to work around some routes that can handle the heavy and wide load. Fortunately, he has an escort vehicle with him already, so that'll help."

"Fantastic."

He continued, "I'm going to drive over myself for a look. I should be there in less than half an hour."

"Thanks again, Alex, we really appreciate it."

When I reached the chief, I told him about the Hauser's willingness to help, and that one machine was on the way.

"Super. Thanks, Dan." He continued, "Deputy Chief Atkins and I were just discussing some of the things we must do to manage this scene. The mayor and the chief of police are on the way. Hopefully, they can handle the press. The police are setting up perimeter barriers. My biggest concern is whether the other tower will come down."

Four members of the police department approached us wearing helmets and bulky vests. Chief Williams said, "This must be the bomb squad."

Everyone shook hands, and the leader of the bomb squad introduced himself as Lieutenant Novella. They each had their name and rank on a patch on their vests.

Lt. Novella asked, "What's your immediate concern Chief?"

"We don't yet know what caused this disaster. If it was a bomb, we need to know and ensure there isn't another one in the other tower about to go off."

Lt. Novella replied, "Most likely, any evidence of a bomb will be at the bottom of the pile. Right now, we can search the remaining tower and canvas the surrounding area for cameras that might have recorded what happened."

"Okay, Lieutenant, have at it." Chief Williams replied, "Keep me posted!"

Deputy Chief Atkins announced a moment later, "We think we have all the people out. They are all in the street next door. We'll need to move them to a shelter before the heat of the day becomes too much."

"Have we found any more survivors?" I inquired.

"Other than the ones from the other tower, no," the chief said, shaking his head. "We are starting to find some dead bodies, however. There's another thing. We are going to need the coroner down here. I would guess they will need a refrigerated truck."

The deputy chief offered, "I'll make that call." He returned to his truck to make a phone call, preferring not to send that request out over the radio.

Just then, a professional-looking, middle-aged lady with dark hair approached us.

"Are you the Chief?" she asked with tears in her eyes.

"Yes, ma'am."

"My name is Diane. I am the property manager here. I just drove into work and cannot believe what I am seeing. I guess you are going to need my help today."

"That's for sure," said Chief Williams. "We think we have everyone evacuated from the other tower, and have them gathered in the street next door. Can you check on them first and find out what they need?" He continued, "We're planning to move them to a shelter soon, but maybe some of them have family in the area and would prefer to go there."

"Yes, I will do that right now," she said, recovering a bit with a task to focus on.

"Thanks. Once you're comfortable with that, we'll need a list of all people in residence here at some point. In both buildings."

"Sure. I'll let you know when I have that together for you."

"Okay, Diane. We'll talk again later. Thank you so much."

When she walked away, I said, "This will be a very traumatic day for her. Maybe we should get a psychologist on the scene to help out. They could help with the residents and also keep an eye out for her."

"Good idea, Dan. When the mayor arrives, I'll speak to him about that."

"Another thought, chief. Do we have any remote microphones or cameras we can drop down in the holes in the rubble?"

"Well, one of these units has that stuff. We have some Go-Pro cameras mounted on extendable selfie sticks to look into second-floor windows during fires. They Bluetooth to a phone or iPad. I'll call out on the radio and see who has them."

Just then, I saw Alex walking toward us. "Excuse me, Chief."

I headed toward Alex and reached for a handshake. "Thanks for coming," I said. "How far away did you have to park?"

"About three blocks. We'll need some help when Ernie gets here with the excavator."

"We can do that. Let's walk around a bit to get your thoughts about site logistics."

"You wanted to be a firefighter ever since we were kids," Alex said, "I'll bet you never imagined a scene like this!"

"You're right about that, Alex. And you always wanted to operate machines; I'll bet you never thought you'd work a scene like this either."

We both shook our heads at the irony.

As we walked, I told him about our fears of the other tower falling and that we were waiting for the bomb squad and the building department to weigh in. I showed him the waste pile we had started along the street on the west side that we hoped could eventually be loaded onto trucks.

"That could work. What concerns me is how little room you have to work. I assume that this is a search-and-rescue operation right now. We do not want to drive an excavator up on the pile. That would just further crush anything underneath it."

I just stood there, nodding my head in agreement.

He continued, "So all we can do is pick along the sides, work with the manual labor, and work our way in that way. I don't see that you have room for more than two machines to work."

Again, I nodded my head. "I see exactly what you mean. But with all this manpower, we need machines to move this rubble out of the way. Any other ideas?"

"How about a crane?" he offered, scratching his head. "It could sit over there next to the other tower, extend the boom over, and start lifting from the center of the pile. I mean, a crane is used to build structures like this. Maybe that's the best way to take them apart."

I tried to envision what he was proposing. I thought lifting debris from the top of the pile made a lot of sense. "I like it. Let's go sell it to the chief."

On our way back to share our idea with Chief Williams, We saw Jim and Carlos carrying two lifeless, broken bodies away from the pile. I saw Alex's face turn gray. Then he turned around and threw up. Christ, this is going to be a tough day.

As we continued walking toward the Chief, we noticed that the mayor and one of his staff were talking to the press on the sidewalk. We also saw the police chief had arrived with more uniformed officers. They were setting up additional crowd control barriers. When we reached the chief, I introduced Alex and explained our thoughts about the crane.

He agreed with our plan and said, "Let me speak to the mayor about approving the expense of a crane. I'll add that to the list of items we need to discuss."

I walked Alex back to the street, and we approached one of the uniforms. I asked him to coordinate clearing the street for the arrival of the excavator that Ernie and Alex would shortly need to unload. Looking around, I could see fire engines as far as the eye could see, and I knew we had created our own traffic jam with huge vehicles. We explained to the uniformed officer that we would need street access for dump trucks to pull up to our discard pile to be loaded and hauled away. I then returned to the pile to see how my team was doing. I found Mikey directing our one excavator, lifting pieces of debris off the pile.

"Are we finding any survivors?" I asked.

"Not yet, but we think we heard some sounds coming from right under this spot. However, we can't hear much with this machine running. How about we set up a plan to work for ten minutes and listen for two?"

"Makes sense to me. Have the cameras made it here yet?"

"Yes," he replied. "Two guys from unit 18 are getting ready to try them."

"Okay. Let's try the two-minute pause to see what we can hear."

Mikey signaled the machine operator to shut down and announced the plan to the other guys working the pile over the radio. We all listened carefully, and after about fifteen seconds, we heard a cry for help coming from the spot right underneath where I was standing. It was a man's voice.

"Everyone, let's spread out and keep listening for anything else," I announced.

It was slow going, climbing on the rubble, so no one got too far. But after another two minutes, we couldn't hear anything. "Okay, let's get back to work," I said. "Let's see if we can open any passage to get a camera down closer to this man underneath us."

I stayed there, working with Mikey, Jim, Donnie, and Carlos. We all still had our respirators on due to the dust we were disturbing. Anything we could pick up, we did, and then threw it in the excavator bucket. Most everything was too large, so we wrapped chains around the pieces the best we could, hooking them on the bucket to be lifted away.

We got one big slab off the pile, which exposed a void about six feet deep.

"Let's get those cameras up here," I called out.

Ian O'Malley and Tom Smith from the 18th had been standing by, ready to go with a camera and an iPad. They climbed up to join us, and we went into another quiet period. Ian held the iPad to monitor the pictures while Tom extended the wand and stuck the camera down into the void, attempting to look into the nooks and crannies that led deeper into the rubble. I was peering over Ian's shoulder when he told Tom to hold it right there. Suddenly, we saw something light blue on the screen.

Ian exclaimed, "We've got something there. See if you can probe a bit deeper. Maybe we can identify it."

As Tom extended it farther, he moved it right and left a bit, limited by the size of the hole.

"I think that is clothing," said Ian. "I can identify a shirt pocket."

"I think you're right," I agreed. "Let's get a microphone and a bullhorn up here. Maybe we can communicate with him."

While waiting for Carlos to get the equipment, we fired up the machine again and lifted pieces off the pile above our discovery. When Carlos returned, we went back to quiet mode. We dropped the microphone on its cord into the hole near the blue shirt. Carlos used earphones to listen, and I used the bullhorn to say, "Hello, can you hear me?"

Carlos claimed he heard a yes, followed by a moan. I announced that we were coming to get him and went silent again. We all looked at Carlos for any other sign of communication.

"The man said, 'I am with my wife. We're being crushed and can't move.'"

I announced over the horn, "Relax the best you can. We are on our way."

We all went back to work with even more energy and determination. I radioed the EMTs and told them what we had. Two of them joined us right away and told me to be very careful and let them examine the couple before lifting the last amount of weight off them. They explained that all kinds of problems can occur when an extreme weight is lifted off a human body—something called hypovolemia caused by the restriction of cellular fluid and the imbalance of sodium, potassium, and other elements when fluids resume flowing. In addition, there could be renal or heart failure and other problems. "Quite simply, it's called crush syndrome," he added.

It took another half an hour of work before we removed enough rubble to see and touch the two survivors. I called the EMTs back to tell them we were ready. The remaining weight was primarily a steel beam with concrete attached that was lying across their hips and midsections. The EMTs checked all their vital signs and set up an IV for each of them, along with oxygen masks.

Meanwhile, we wrapped chains around the beam, preparing to lift it. They signaled they were ready, and we hooked the chains up to the bucket and signaled to the operator to start lifting. He went really slow and easy, watching the faces of the EMTs for direction. They signaled all clear, and he lifted the beam away, swinging it around to the discard pile.

We helped the EMTs get the injured couple on stretchers and carried them down to the ambulances. On the way, they asked us if we had found their niece. They told us her name was Jackie and were quite distraught about finding her.

"Is she a young teenager with dark hair?"

"Oh yes, please tell us she is okay!" the woman begged.

"As a matter of fact, I spoke to her myself after pulling her out of the rubble. She's at the hospital but should be fine."

"Oh, thank God. Bless you."

Once they were settled in for the ride, off they went.

"Okay, two more lives saved!" I exclaimed with a feeling of joy.

It was now after nine a.m. A coffee truck had come to the site, and my team took a short break. We had been working for eight hours straight with nothing more than water. Not only was the work extremely physical, but it was emotionally draining as well. I figured it would be good for the guys to catch their breath and get coffee and an egg sandwich. With two coffee cups in hand, I walked over to the chief.

"Bless you, Dan," he said as he took a sip. He brought me up to date on his talk with the mayor. He told me that the crane was approved, that the mayor's office would arrange for it to arrive this morning, and that a psychologist was on the way from the hospital. He explained that the bomb squad had found nothing so far, and we were still waiting for the building inspectors to complete their evaluation of the tower, which could take most of the day. Other surrounding fire departments would be sending in men to relieve us after this afternoon. "Oh," he added. "I have a press conference scheduled for ten o'clock with the mayor and the police chief."

"Lucky you," I said, my voice dripping with sarcasm.

By now, Ernie had arrived with his excavator and had joined the effort. The highway department was sending over a few dump trucks that we could start loading upon their arrival. When the crane showed up, we'd really be able to make some progress. Now that everyone was evacuated from the other tower, Captain Sanchez and his guys from Unit 18 had joined the search through the rubble pile.

As it stood, we had rescued three people and found six dead bodies that would be identifiable. There were also additional body parts in pieces or crushed beyond recognition. Because of the extreme weight and energy released during the collapse, much of what was in the building, including human bodies, had been pulverized into dust. This was my first time working on a high-rise collapse, but I had read many of the accounts from 9/11 and attended some continuing-ed seminars, and this pulverization is what they found to be the case. It was really beyond imagination.

My train of thought reminded me that everyone should be wearing some form of breathing protection. I went into the bins on the side of the truck and grabbed a handful of N-95 masks. I then approached both machine operators and gave a couple of masks to each of them. Of course, the EMTs already had their own protection.

Suddenly, I felt my phone vibrating in my pocket. I took it out and saw my daughter's face on the screen. "Hi, Kate."

"Hi, Daddy. Are you at the building collapse?" she asked, her voice trembling slightly.

"Yes, I am, honey. I've been here all night. I was about to text you that I can't pick you up from lacrosse practice this afternoon. Can you get a ride home?" Typically, my two-day shifts end at noon. After eating a quick bite, I liked to swing by her school and watch her practices, then give her a lift home.

She replied, "Sure, that's fine. But more importantly, how are you doing? I heard it's just horrible."

"Yeah, it's pretty bad; I'm trying to focus on the task at hand without thinking about the horror. I'm hoping to be home in time for dinner. Some other teams should be coming in this afternoon to relieve us."

"Okay, take care of yourself," she replied. "I'll make your favorite dinner tonight. Bye, Daddy."

"Bye, honey."

Kate was a high school senior and the lacrosse team captain. We lost her mother four years earlier to a sudden brain aneurysm. My late wife had complained of a bad headache like nothing she'd ever experienced. I got her in the car and headed for the hospital. She never even made it out of the vehicle. As we drove, her head fell against the side window. When we got to the emergency room, the doctors concluded, "We're sorry, Mr. Crawford. She is gone. There is nothing we can do."

As shocking as that was to me, I think it was tougher on Kate. We clung to one another and cried for the first few hours, and then we walked around in a fog for a few days. She would sit next to me and hug my arm with her head on my shoulder, sometimes sobbing and sometimes sleeping. Here she was, becoming a teenager and having to do it without her mother. We held it together the best we could with the help of a family counselor. After a few months of grieving, we decided that Kate should see a psychologist of her own, which seems to have worked out for her. She'd been seeing her once a month ever since and, hopefully, found it easier to talk about things she would be uncomfortable discussing with her father.

Seeing Kate's face on my phone screen reminded me of her mother and how much I miss her. She had the same light hazel eyes as her mother; sometimes they looked green, and sometimes they looked gold—truly remarkable.

It was now nearly noon. The press conference had broken up, and I could no longer see the mayor. Reporters were still hanging around, hoping for a bit of news or a photo-op. I headed back to the pile and teamed up with Bruno to clear debris by hand. The crane had arrived and was being set up on the street.

After deploying his stabilizers and leveling up, he extended the boom over the pile. Mikey had already spoken with the crane operator and reviewed the plan of action. The operator would control the whole thing with a remote that hung around his neck. He would stand on the pile in a stable area with a clear view of his crane, the items to be picked up, and the discard pile. With the operator in place, Ernie would focus on loading the dump trucks from the discard pile. We were running out of room to work, but Mikey seemed to be in control of orchestrating the operation.

For the next few hours, this was our routine. We continued with our strategy of working for ten minutes and listening for two minutes, but we found no more survivors and heard no more cries for help. We did come across some more human remains, though not as many as I had anticipated. The coroner managed to keep up by running back and forth to the morgue.

I wondered who would take over when the shifts would change. We all knew we would go beyond our usual end of the shift at noon. I hoped we could hang in until five or six. The other shift from our station arrived mid-afternoon, led by Lieutenant Matt Danzinger. Knowing they would go all night, they initially spent the first ten minutes familiarizing themselves with the site and observing how we worked it. Then, they joined us on the pile and helped us with the manual labor and working with the excavators and the crane. More firefighters from the next shifts started to show up, and we were running out of room to work, and the machines could not keep up.

I approached Lt. Danzinger. He was my equal in rank and experience. We joined the force around the same time and had worked together for many years. I knew he was a good man, and the other guys respected him. I asked him how he felt about taking charge of the coordination with the crane and machine operators.

"I can handle it if you show me the ropes."

"Better yet, let me have Mike Lopes show you what we're doing. He's been running the show all day," I replied.

We walked to where Mikey was working, and Matt greeted him.

"Matt is willing to take over for you if you show him how," I got straight to the point.

"Certainly. Have you ever worked with excavators or cranes before?"

"A long time ago," replied Matt. "Back in college, I spent summers with a concrete foundation crew."

"Great, how about we work together until you get the hang of it."

"Okay, thanks, Mike. Let's do it."

I left the two of them to it and headed back down to see if I could find the chief. I was comforted knowing someone could take charge when we went home, and I hoped the chief agreed.

When I found Chief Williams, he was speaking with Diane, the property manager. It was nearly four o'clock, and she was getting ready to go home. She told us that all the displaced residents from the standing tower were accounted for and placed at the shelter or with friends or relatives. She told us she had the residents list mainly together and would complete it by the morning. The three of us exchanged phone numbers, and she asked if there was anything else she could do.

"Not tonight," the Chief said. "You go home and take care of yourself. We know how traumatic all of this is. We'll see you again tomorrow."

"Goodnight," Diane sighed, clearly exhausted and eager to get home to the comfort of her family.

"Goodnight," we answered, hoping she could get some rest tonight.

We saw Lt. Novella approaching, and we were anxious to hear what he had to say.

"The other tower is clear, with no evidence of explosives anywhere. We have identified a few cameras on surrounding buildings and one at the traffic light. We're reviewing the record-ings now," he reported.

"Thanks, Lieutenant; let me know as soon as you have a finding," the chief replied.

Then, I told the chief that Lt. Danzinger would take charge of the machine coordination on the pile.

"Sounds good, Dan. I plan to take a room at the Resi-dence Inn across the street to get some shut-eye yet still be close by in case I am needed. When do you plan to head home?"

"Pretty soon. I just want to take another tour of the pile to check on my guys and see if we can keep the machines running overnight. I'm hoping the operators have some replacements coming in. They've already put in a long day."

"Okay, the mayor told me that Public Works would send another operator after five. Update me again before you leave, Dan."

"Will do."

I first spoke to the crane operator. He told me his boss would arrive in a while and planned to keep it going as long as he had enough light to see safely. I was happy to hear that people were still thinking about safety after being tired. I checked in with Ernie on the other excavator, and he told me Alex would return after dinner to relieve him. I updated Mikey about the plans to keep the machines going all night. I asked him how it was going with Lt. Danzinger.

"Great," he replied. "He gets it and should do just fine."

I then spoke with Matt and told him I was leaving the pile in his hands for the night. I filled him in on the machine operators and asked him to see the chief when he had a free moment. "He'll want to tell you how to keep in touch with him."

"Will do," Matt said.

We shook hands, and I climbed back down off the pile to report back to the chief.

"It sounds like we have replacements to keep the machines running for the night," I told him. "I'm going to shove off if it's okay with you, Chief."

"Sure, Dan. Get some rest."

"I hope I can. See you bright and early."

Carlos, Bruno, and I bummed a ride back to the station with one of the uniformed police officers in his cruiser. He offered us water bottles from a cooler, and we all chugged them down like we had just walked the Sahara Desert. Once back at the station, I could barely get out of the car. I was exhausted, and my legs were not working properly. We all said goodnight, got in our cars, and headed home. *I'll never forget this day!*

It was six-thirty by the time I walked into the house. From the smell, I could tell Kate was making pot roast with stewed vegetables, potatoes, and gravy—her mom's recipe—my favorite.

"It smells fantastic in here, Katie," I said, giving her a long hug.

"Thanks, Daddy. I started it as soon as I got home. It should be ready in an hour."

"Great. That will give me time to get these clothes off and take a shower."

"Go do it, Daddy. You're covered in dust; I've never seen you this dirty!"

Half an hour later, I walked down the stairs, clean but exhausted. I collapsed into my recliner and took a few deep breaths.

"I made you a Manhattan, Daddy," Kate announced as she carried it over in a martini glass filled to the brim, careful not to spill it. "Do you want to talk about it?"

"I don't think so, honey. It's all too raw, and I'm afraid if I open that door, it will overwhelm me. I just want to sit here, enjoy this drink, and watch you cook. Did I tell you it smells fantastic?"

"Yes, you did, Daddy," she smiled. "It should be ready as soon as I finish the gravy."

I took a few sips of my drink and felt the relief spread through my body. I watched my daughter prepare dinner and asked about her day, much like I used to do with her mother for so many years. Kate told me about the upcoming graduation ceremony, her lacrosse practice, and the final game of the season on Saturday. This was really the most enjoyable part of each day for me. It would not be long until she was off to college, and I would be cooking for myself each night—or bringing home take-out. I was happy that she got a partial scholarship at Florida Atlantic University, just an hour away, so I could at least see her on some weekends.

"It's ready," she said as she set out the plates.

We both sat down at the dinner table and thoroughly enjoyed our meal. After, I helped her clear the table and load the dishwasher.

"Leave the pans in the sink," she said. "I'll do them later…"

She then set out two mugs of decaf coffee and a few oatmeal cookies. We sipped on our hot drinks and munched on our dessert, making idle conversation until I declared I was going to bed. "Thank you for the lovely meal, honey."

"Good night, Daddy," she replied, kissing me on the cheek.

The following day, I was woken by an alarm again. This time, it was one I had set myself for six a.m. Sitting up in bed, I checked my emails and messages. I saw that Chief Williams had sent a text that he had arranged for all rescue personnel to have free parking at the garage next to the Residence Inn. That was good news—I could drive directly there without going to the station first.

I took the time to shave and leisurely get dressed before heading downstairs for coffee. I saw a note from Kate that she had made me a pot roast sandwich for lunch and had put it in the fridge. I sat in front of the TV and watched the news as I sipped my coffee and ate a bowl of cereal. The news, of course, was all about the collapse. They replayed video from the news conference with the Mayor, then showed footage of us working with the excavators and crane. There was a brief glimpse of dead bodies being carted away; then, I saw a close-up of myself directing an excavator. Overall, I think the coverage showed an accurate account of yesterday's events.

It was time for me to go, and I headed out for the drive into the city, wondering how I would physically and emotionally respond to a second day of this disaster.

After parking in the garage, I saw the chief standing where I left him the night before. He was looking over some blueprints on the hood of his Tahoe.

"Good morning, Chief."

"Good morning, Dan."

"How did the guys make out last night?" I asked.

"Well, we found four more survivors. It looks like Lieutenant Danzinger was able to keep it all going overnight. We had no injuries among all of us working."

"That's great to hear."

"The Sheriff's department will send a K-9 unit with cadaver dogs this morning to help with the search. Can you coordinate with them when they arrive?"

"Sure thing, Chief."

After a moment, he continued. "There are a couple of engineers in the other tower right now. The building department called them in to confirm their findings from yesterday. We should know shortly if that building is stable. They left me an original set of blueprints from forty years ago, and I am currently trying to get familiar with them, although I am a bit rusty at reading prints."

"I know what you mean," I agreed. "It gives me a headache just looking at them."

"Yeah, I intend to leave any decision-making to the engineers."

We then saw Lt. Novella approaching. We waited patiently to hear what he had to say. "We were able to review video and sound from four recordings and have determined there was no explosion preceding the collapse. No sound or flash of light. The best video was from the parking garage across the street. That camera showed the inside of this parking garage, and there was a sudden flood of water from above about two minutes before the collapse. After comparing that scene to the blueprints, I think the swimming pool gave way first, followed by the pool deck, then the rest."

"So this was a structural failure, nothing more nefarious?"

"I believe so, Chief. I am not an engineer, so take that for what it's worth, but I'll provide the building department with copies of the footage for their engineers to review."

"Thanks for the good work, Lieutenant."

"Good luck here, guys; I hope you find more survivors," he said as he walked away.

I saw Mikey and the other guys heading up the pile. I joined them and approached Matt to get brought up to speed. "I heard you had four more survivors last night," I said.

"Yes. Two we found together that were pretty stable. The other two we found separately, and they were both in rough shape. I hope they make it."

"We're ready to resume the mission if you and your guys want to get some sleep."

With a sigh, Matt replied, "Yeah, we're all in the middle of our two-day shift, so we'll just ride back to the station together for some rest. See you this evening, Dan."

I relayed the information from the bomb squad to the rest of my team, along with Matt's, and the word spread around the site.

As I watched Matt descend the pile, I heard a groan over the radio and saw a commotion just below me. I rushed down and saw Carlos with one leg out of sight in a hole in the rubble and his other leg twisted awkwardly underneath his torso on a concrete slab. He was writhing in pain. Seeing his leg in such an unnatural position made me think he must have torn muscles or tendons in his groin if not broken bones. Matt came back up to help me lift Carlos by the shoulders straight up out of the hole. Now, both legs were hanging underneath him, and he was in excruciating pain.

Matt called for paramedics on the radio, and they arrived within seconds. The paramedics cut away his pants near his groin, exposing a large hematoma that was forming. Carlos was doing everything he could not to scream. They called for a stretcher and gave Carlos a morphine injection to relieve his pain. Within a minute, he began to calm down while the stretcher was being delivered up the pile. When they had him on the stretcher and were carrying him down, I thought to myself, *Just an hour ago, the chief told me we had no injuries overnight!* I followed them down and spoke to Carlos, trying to comfort him, as they loaded him in an ambulance and drove away. I was shaken but returned to the pile to resume work.

At about thirty hours in, we were fortunate that it took that long for our first firefighter to become injured. Climbing around an unstable pile with jagged steel everywhere was a recipe for injury. While reflecting, I paused to take in the entire scene and assess our progress. As slow as the whole process seemed, we'd made a noticeable dent in the pile.

We had a fresh operator on the crane, and the city excavator was on the scene. I saw that Ernie was back on his machine, and the dump trucks had started running again. So far that morning, we had found no signs of life. We would keep up hope for another three days. After one hundred hours, it was unlikely that anyone could survive without water.

I saw the K-9 unit arrive and release three dogs from the truck. The dogs sat beside each other, eagerly awaiting a command. I recognized Andy Carvalho as their handler; we had worked together a few years ago on a search for missing children. I walked down to greet him, and he introduced me to Claymore and Sarge, two Belgian Malinois, and Kemba, a Border Collie. All remained sitting, with their eyes locked on Andy, still waiting for a command.

I asked Andy, "Why was I expecting bloodhounds?"

"We use bloodhounds on level ground and in the Glades; they are considered field cadaver dogs. These are disaster cadaver dogs trained for a rubble pile. Claymore and Sarge are retired military; they served in Iraq and are experienced with this sort of scene. And Kemba is just about the smartest, most agile dog I've ever worked with," he explained. "Where would you like us to start?"

"I'll let you lead them, or I should say, they lead you. If I knew where the bodies were, we would already be digging there."

Andy looked the dogs in the eye and said, "Go."

The three ran off together and climbed up the pile with a speed no human could match. They searched and smelled, sticking their noses into holes. It wasn't long before they assembled in one spot and started barking. Andy and I had been following behind and joined the dogs a minute later.

I called over the radio for any of my team members who weren't already occupied with a suspected survivor. Mikey and Bruno headed our way along with the crane operator. Once we started removing debris from this new spot, Andy took the two Malinois with him to begin a new search elsewhere, leaving Kemba behind with us. As we removed pieces by hand, the crane operator prepared chains to wrap around a massive concrete slab. When he was satisfied it was secure, he lowered the boom to grab the hook and connect it to the chains. Slowly, he began to lift it, again testing that it was secure. Then he lifted it up and out of the way and swung it over to the discard pile. Kemba climbed down a little deeper and started barking again at a new hole that had been exposed. My team returned to removing whatever pieces they could by hand and placed them in a three-cubic-yard container that the crane would pick up and carry away. All this went slowly and deliberately, but the dog seemed convinced we were working in the right direction. Again, we came across something too big, and the crane operator prepared to lower the hook while my team connected the chains this time.

Once connected, he slowly lifted, and when we were confident with the grip, he raised and swung it away. We could now see a human leg, and Kemba remained there, focused on it. As we cleared away more debris, we could see two motionless bodies. I called the paramedics over to check for life. They got down on their bellies and reached down to touch them.

After a moment, one said, "Sorry, Dan, these two are stone cold."

It took us about ten minutes to manually get the bodies out and place them in a container for the crane operator to lift out and lower down to the coroner.

Kemba had now worked her way to another spot about thirty feet away and started barking again. My team made our way over there and resumed working. With Kemba's encour-agement, we found another person about a half hour later. This time, a hand reached out to us. Kemba went down and started licking the hand, and it looked like the hand petted the dog's nose. I called Kemba back out of the hole, and my team worked in earnest, manually clearing away the rubble, knowing we had found someone alive. I again called the paramedics over, and this time, they put an oxygen mask on the survivor and loaded her on a stretcher. The two paramedics carried the stretcher down the pile and placed it in an ambulance to be rushed to the hospital.

I notified Andy over the radio that Kemba had just saved a life. He came rushing over to praise her, which the dog eagerly relished.

As the day continued, the dogs proved worth their weight in gold. They focused our work on certain spots that other-wise would have been just random or from the outside in. The coffee truck showed up at lunchtime, so my team took a break. Many of us sat on the running boards of our fire engine, chat-ting and eating, while I sipped on a coffee and enjoyed my pot roast sandwich.

After lunch, we continued our work with the dogs. They found more bodies but, unfortunately, no more survivors.

Chief Williams stopped by in the afternoon and gave us some updated information.

"First, about Carlos: he has a torn groin muscle, but surgery was successful, and he should recover completely in a few months."

We all let out a sigh of relief. He then told us that the other tower was not in immediate danger of falling, according to the engineers, and also that the building department posted it as condemned, never to be occupied again. He also told us that Diane, the property manager, had supplied him with a list of all residents of both towers and marked the list for who was accounted for and their current location.

"Do you plan to have her identify the bodies?" I asked.

"I hope she doesn't have to do that," he replied, shaking his head. "Maybe as a last resort, if the coroner or the medical staff have no other way to do it. I think all the injured survivors have been identified already."

After lunch, we all climbed back up the pile and resumed working with the dogs. The overhead sun was relentless. We were all soaked with sweat and working zombie-like with our heads down on the repetitive task of clearing debris. We focused on keeping hydrated, and Andy made sure his dogs had plenty to drink by filling bowls with bottled water.

We found no more survivors that afternoon but came across some gruesome human remains, crushed beyond recognition. Each time, we placed the matter in containers so the coroner could identify it through DNA analysis.

The following day went much like the last. We kept working in the heat and the dust. The work became drudgery, and any joy we had felt from locating a survivor had long since disappeared. Climbing around on an unstable rubble pile had taken a physical toll on our bodies, and the pain in our legs and backs had become overwhelming.

We came across the lower half of a man's body separated at the waist. The torso was nowhere to be seen. I noticed a wallet in the back pocket; his driver's license identified him as Robert P. Randazzo. I made sure the coroner's team kept the wallet with the remains.

And so it went for the next ten days—with the search and rescue phase over, the recovery and clean-up phase began. With the possibility of finding a survivor no longer realistic, the depression from handling human remains overcame us all.

When we neared the bottom of the pile, the engineers hired by the city showed up again. They spoke with the chief and explained that they were there to inspect the debris before it was hauled away. They hung around the discard pile wearing hard hats, examining the pieces as the crane and the excavators dropped them. They were looking to find the cause of the collapse. If any piece of steel or concrete looked suspect, they would have it placed on a flatbed trailer. To the untrained eye, it all looked like a bunch of rubble, but just by looking at it, they could tell if it showed signs of rust or decay that had occurred over time before the collapse. They were confident their fellow engineers would know what brought down this building in the coming weeks and months.

With help from neighboring fire departments, we transitioned to eight-hour shifts, which was a tremendous break for all of us. A person can only do twelve-plus hour shifts for so long. In the end, there were only eight survivors; ninety were presumed dead. I say presumed because there were only twenty identifiable bodies recovered.

Less than a month later, a demolition team came in with dynamite charges and dropped the other tower within its own footprint. The Oceanside Towers were now a part of history.

EPILOGUE

Hannah and Bob Osborne were horrified when they heard of the collapse at Oceanside. Many friends and acquaintances lost their lives; some went days before being identified, some never. It was sheer luck and fate, they both agreed, that kept them from plunging to their deaths while sleeping that fateful night. They wondered about the people who bought unit 505 and then had to stop because it was too haunting.

When Karen called Hannah from the hospital two days later, she and Bob were overjoyed that Jim, Karen, and her niece, Jackie, had been miraculously rescued.

According to various news reports, a preliminary investigation revealed a "severe strength deficiency" in the pool deck. There is a suggestion that the pool deck supporting columns lacked sufficient strength and that perhaps additions such as planters and heavy pavers were not initially accounted for. What is certain, however, is that over the last few years, the columns and beams had not been repaired or viewed as a priority when they clearly showed signs of deterioration. Some consider it negligence on the part of the Board of Directors. Surely, the onset of the Covid pandemic contributed to the delays.

The full investigation is expected to cost around twenty-two million dollars and should be complete in 2025.

In June of 2023, plans were submitted to build a new twelve-story condominium on the site where the catastrophe occurred.

THE END

ACKNOWLEDGMENTS

A first novel is a daunting yet rewarding experience. I must thank all those who helped me along the way, especially Mike Preston, who provided technical guidance for the first responder's story. I want to thank all those who helped with editing and my friends and family who supported me along the way. And finally, I dedicate this to the love of my life, my wife Beth, whose everlasting encouragement makes everything possible.

Follow the author at larryterhaar.com